SOMEONE WAS TRYING TO STRAND HIM—EONS IN EARTH'S PAST

I was walking along the beach when I heard the *boom!* of gunfire. Slipping and sliding my way upslope, I crashed through a screen of cycads at the crest.

Below me, two warcars in the fifty-ton range were parked on the sand a few hundred yards from the station. As I watched, almost invisible fire jetted from their guns. I dropped flat in time to get the shock wave against my ribs: a kick from a buried giant.

I came up at a dead run, spitting sand and not thinking too clearly, but absolutely, unconditionally convinced that whatever was going on down there, the only Timecast booth this side of the Pleistocene was inside the station, and the nearer I got to it before they got me, the happier I'd die . . .

"Tautly written and endless suspense. An excellent book."   —*Columbus Dispatch*

KEITH LAUMER

DINOSAUR BEACH

BAEN
SCIENCE FICTION
BOOKS

This book is affectionately dedicated to
Anne Taylor, R.N.

A Baen Book

Baen Publishing Enterprises
260 Fifth Avenue
New York, N.Y. 10001

First Baen printing, July 1986

ISBN: 0-671-65581-7

Cover art by Tom Kidd

Printed in the United States of America

Distributed by
SIMON & SCHUSTER
TRADE PUBLISHING GROUP
1230 Avenue of the Americas
New York, N.Y. 10020

◊ **1** ◊

It was a pleasant summer evening. We were sitting on the porch swing, Lisa and I, watching the last of the pink fade out of the sky and listening to Fred Hunnicut pushing a lawn mower over his weed crop next door. A cricket in the woodwork started up his fiddle, sounding businesslike and full of energy. A car rattled by, its weak yellow headlights pushing shadows along the brick street and reflecting in the foliage of the sycamores that arched over the pavement. Somewhere a radio sang about harbor lights.

A pleasant evening, a pleasant place. I hated to leave it. But I took a breath of crisp air lightly laced with leafsmoke and newcut grass and got to my feet.

Lisa looked up at me. She had a heart-shaped face, and a short nose, and big, wide-spaced eyes and the prettiest smile in the world. Even the tiny scar on her cheekbone only added to her charm: the flaw that makes perfection perfect.

"Think I'll walk down to Simon's for some beer," I said.

"Dinner will be ready when you get back, darlin'," she said, and smiled the smile. "Baked ham and corn on the cob."

She stood and moved against me all in one fluid dancer's motion, and her lips touched my ear.

I went down the steps and paused on the walk to look back and see her silhouetted against the lighted screen door, slim and graceful.

"Hurry back, darlin'," she said, and waved and was gone.

Gone forever.

She didn't know I wouldn't be coming back.

◇ **2** ◇

A streetcar clacked and sparked past the inter-
section, a big toy with cutout heads pasted against
the row of little square windows. Horns tooted.
Traffic lights winked. People hurried past, on their
way home after a long day in the store or the office
or the cement plant. I bucked the tide, not hurrying, not dawdling. I had plenty of time. That was
one lesson I'd learned. You can't speed it up, you
can't slow it down. Sometimes you can avoid it
completely, but that's a different matter.

These reflections carried me the four blocks to
the taxi stand on Delaware. I climbed in the back
of a Reo that looked as if it should have been
retired a decade back and told the man where I
wanted to go. He gave me a look that wondered
what a cleancut young fellow like me wanted in
that part of town. He opened his mouth to say it,
and I said, "Make it under seven minutes and
there's five in it."

He dropped the flag and almost tore the clutch
out of the Reo getting away from the curb. All the
way there he watched me in the mirror, mentally

3

trying out various approaches to the questions he wanted to ask. I saw the neon letters, the color of red-hot iron, half a block ahead and pulled him over, shoved the five into his hand and was on my way before he'd figured out just how to phrase it.

It was a shabby-genteel cocktail bar, the class of the neighborhood, with two steps down into a room that had been a nice one once, well before Prohibition. The dark paneled walls hadn't suffered much from the years, and aside from a patina of grime, the figured ceiling was passable; but the maroon carpet had a wide, worn strip that meandered like a jungle trail across to the long bar, branching off to get lost among the chair legs. The solid leather seats in the booths along the wall had lost a lot of their color, and some of their stitching had been patched with tape; and nobody had bothered to polish away the rings left by generations of beers on the oak tabletops. I took a booth halfway back, with a little brass lamp with a parchment shade and a framed print on the wall showing somebody's champion steeplechaser circa 1910. The clock over the bar said 7:44.

I ordered a grenadine from a waitress who'd been in her prime about the same time as the bar. She brought it and I took a sip and a man slid into the seat across from me. He took a couple of breaths as if he'd just finished a brisk lap around the track, and said, "Do you mind?" He waved the glass in his hand at the room, which was crowded, but not that crowded.

I took my time looking him over. He had a soft, round face, very pale blue eyes, the kind of head that ought to be bald but was covered with a fine blond down, like baby chicken feathers. He was wearing a striped shirt with the open collar laid back over a bulky plaid jacket with padded shoulders and wide lapels. His neck was smooth-skinned, and too thin for his head. The hand that was holding the glass was small and well-lotioned, with short, immaculately manicured nails. He wore a big, cumbersome-looking gold ring with a glass ruby big enough for a paperweight on his left index finger. The whole composition looked a little out of tune, as if it had been put together in a hurry by someone with more important things on his mind.

"Please don't get the wrong impression," he said. His voice was like the rest of him: not feminine enough for a woman, but nothing you'd associate with a room full of cigar smoke, either.

"It's vital that I speak to you, Mr. Ravel," he went on, talking fast, getting it said before it was too late. "It's a matter of great importance . . . to your future." He paused to check the effect of his words: a tentative sort of pause, as if he might jump either way, depending on my reaction.

I said, "My future, eh? I wasn't sure I had one."

He liked that; I could see it in the change in the glitter of his eyes. "Oh, yes," he said, and nodded comfortably. "Yes indeed." He took a quick swallow from the glass and lowered it and caught and held my eyes, smiling an elusive little smile. "And I might add that your future is—or can be—a great deal larger than your past."

"Have we met somewhere?" I asked him.

He shook his head. "I know this doesn't make a great deal of sense to you just now—but time is of the essence. Please listen——"

"I'm listening, Mr.—what was the name?"

"It really doesn't matter, Mr. Ravel. I don't enter into the matter at all except as the bearer of a message. I was assigned to contact you and deliver certain information."

"Assigned?"

He shrugged.

I reached across and caught the wrist of the hand that was holding the glass. It was as smooth and soft as a baby's. I applied a small amount of pressure. Some of the drink slopped on the edge of the table and into his lap. He tensed a little, as if he wanted to stand, but I pressed him back. "Let me play too," I said. "Let's go back to where you were telling me about your assignment. I find that sort of intriguing. Who thinks I'm important enough to assign a smooth cookie like you to snoop on?" I grinned at him while he got his smile fixed up and back in place, a little bent now, but still working.

"Mr. Ravel—what would you say if I told you that I am a member of a secret organization of supermen?"

"What would you expect me to say?"

"That I'm insane," he said promptly. "That's why I'd hoped to skirt the subject and go directly to the point. Mr. Ravel, your life is in danger."

I let that hang in the air between us.

"In precisely—" he glanced down at the watch strapped English-style to the underside of his free wrist "—one and one-half minutes a man will enter this establishment. He will be dressed in a costume of black, and will carry a cane—ebony, with a silver head. He will go to the fourth stool at the bar, order a straight whiskey, drink it, turn, raise the cane, and fire three lethal darts into your chest."

I took another swallow of my drink. It was the real stuff; one of the compensations of the job.

"Neat," I said. "What does he do for an encore?"

My little man looked a bit startled. "You jape, Mr. Ravel? I'm speaking of your death. Here. In a matter of seconds!" He leaned across the table to throw this at me, with quite a lot of spit.

"Well, I guess that's that," I said, and let go his arm and raised my glass to him. "Don't go spending a lot of money on a fancy funeral."

It was his turn to grab me. His fat little hand closed on my arm with more power than I'd given him credit for.

"I've been telling you what will happen—*unless* you act at once to avert it!"

"Aha. That's where that big future you mentioned comes in."

"Mr. Ravel—you must leave here at once." He fumbled in a pocket of his coat, brought out a card with an address printed on it: 356 Colvin Court.

"It's an old building, very stable, quite near here. There's an exterior wooden staircase, quite safe. Go to the third floor. A room marked with the numeral 9 is at the back. Enter the room and wait."

"Why should I do all that?" I asked him, and pried his fingers loose from my sleeve.

"In order to save your life!" He sounded a little wild now, as if things weren't working out quite right for him. That suited me fine. I had a distinct feeling that what was right for him might not be best for me and my big future.

"Where'd you get my name?" I asked him.

"Please—time is short. Won't you simply trust me?"

"The name's a phony," I said. "I gave it to a Bible salesman yesterday. Made it up on the spot.

You're not in the book-peddling racket, are you, Mr. Ah?"

"Does that matter more than your life?"

"You're mixed up, pal. It's not my life we're dickering for. It's yours."

His earnest look went all to pieces. He was still trying to reassemble it when the street door opened and a man in a black overcoat, black velvet collar, black homburg, and carrying a black swagger stick walked in.

"You see?" My new chum slid the whisper across the table like a dirty picture. "Just as I said. You'll have to act swiftly now, Mr. Ravel, before he sees you——"

"Your technique is slipping," I said. "He had me pat right down to my shoe size before he was halfway through the door." I brushed his hand away and slid out of the booth. The man in black had gone across to the bar and taken the fourth stool, without looking my way. I picked my way between the tables and took the stool on his left.

He didn't look at me, not even when my elbow brushed his side a little harder than strict etiquette allowed. If there was a gun in his pocket, I couldn't feel it. He had propped the cane against his knees, the big silver head an inch or two from his hand. I leaned a little toward him.

"Watch it, the caper's blown," I said about eight inches from his ear.

He took it calmly. His head turned slowly until it was facing me. He had a high, narrow forehead, hollow cheeks, white lines around his nostrils against gray skin. His eyes looked like little black stones.

"Are you addressing me?" he said in a voice with a chill like Scott's last camp on the icecap.

"Who is he?" I said in a tone that suggested that

a couple of smart boys ought to be able to get together and swap confidences.

"Who?" No thaw yet.

"The haberdasher's delight with the hands you hate to touch," I said. "The little guy I was sitting with. He's waiting over in the booth to see how it turns out." I let him have a sample of my frank and open smile.

"You've made an error," Blackie said, and turned away.

"Don't feel bad," I said. "Nobody's perfect. The way I see it—why don't we get together and talk it over—the three of us?"

That got to him; his head jerked—about a millionth of an inch. He slid off his stool, picked up his hat. My foot touched the cane as he reached for it; it fell with a lot of clatter. I accidentally put a foot on it while picking it up for him. Something made a small crunching sound.

"Oops," I said, "sorry and all that," and handed it over. He grabbed it and headed for the men's room. I almost watched him too long; from the corner of my eye I saw my drinking buddy sliding toward the street exit. I caught him a few yards along the avenue, eased him over against the wall. He fought as well as you can fight when you don't want to attract the attention of the passersby.

"Tell me things," I said. "After I bought the mindreading act, what was next?"

"You fool—you're not out of danger yet! I'm trying to save your life—have you no sense of gratitude?"

"If you only knew, chum. What makes it worth the trouble? My suit wouldn't fit you—and the cash in my pockets wouldn't pay cab fare over to

Colvin Court and back. But I guess I wouldn't have been coming back."

"Let me go! We must get off the street!" He tried to kick my ankle, and I socked him under the ribs hard enough to fold him against me wheezing like a bagpipe. The weight made me take a quick step back and I heard a flat *whup!* like a silenced pistol and heard the whicker that a bullet makes when it passes an inch from your ear. There was a deep doorway a few feet away. We made it in one jump. My little pal tried to wreck my knee, and I had to bruise his shins a little.

"Take it easy," I said. "That slug changes things. Quiet down and I'll let go your neck."

He nodded as well as he could with my thumb where it was, and I let up on him. He did some hard breathing and tugged at his collar. His round face looked a bit lopsided now, and the China-blue eyes had lost their baby stare. I made a little production of levering back the hammer of my Mauser, waiting for what came next.

Two or three minutes went past like geologic ages.

"He's gone," the little man said in a flat voice. "They'll chalk this up as an abort and try again. You've escaped nothing, merely postponed it."

"Sufficient unto the day and all that sort of thing," I said. "Let's test the water. You first." I nudged him forward with the gun. Nobody shot at him. I risked a look. No black overcoats in sight.

"Where's your car?" I asked. He nodded toward a black Marmon parked across the street. I walked him across and waited while he slid in under the wheel, then I got in the back. There were other parked cars, and plenty of dark windows for a sniper to work from, but nobody did.

"Any booze at your place?" I said.

"Why—yes—of course." He tried not to look pleased.

He drove badly, like a middle-aged widow after six lessons. We clashed gears and ran stoplights across town to the street he had named. It was a poorly lit macadam dead end that rose steeply toward a tangle of telephone poles at the top. The house was tall and narrow, slanted against the sky, the windows black and empty. He pulled into a drive that was two strips of cracked concrete with weeds in the middle, led the way back along the side of the house past the wooden steps he'd mentioned, used a key on a side door. It resisted a little, then swung in on warped linoleum and the smell of last week's cabbage soup. I followed him in and stopped to listen to some dense silence.

"Don't be concerned," the little man said. "There's no one here." He led me along a passage a little wider than my elbows, past a tarnished mirror, a stand full of furled umbrellas, and a hat tree with no hats, up steep steps with black rubber matting held in place by tarnished brass rods. The flooring creaked on the landing. A tall clock was stopped with the hands at ten past three. We came out in a low-ceilinged hall with flowery brown wallpaper and dark-painted doors made visible by the pale light coming through a curtained window at the end.

He found number 9, put an ear against it, opened up and ushered me in.

It was a small bedroom with a hard-looking double bed under a chenille spread, a brown wooden dresser with a string doily, a straight chair with wire to hold the legs together, a rocker that didn't match, an oval hooked rug in various shades of dried mud, a hanging fixture in the center of the ceiling with three small bulbs, one of which worked.

"Some class," I said. "You must have come into dough."

"Just temporary quarters," he said off-handedly. He placed the chairs in a cozy *tête-à-tête* arrangement under the light, offered me the rocker, and perched on the edge of the other.

"Now," he said, and put his fingertips together comfortably, like a pawnbroker getting ready to bid low on distress merchandise, "I suppose you want to hear all about the man in black, how I knew just when he'd appear, and so on."

"Not especially," I said. "What I'm wondering is what made you think you could get away with it."

"I'm afraid I don't quite understand," he said, and cocked his head sideways.

"It was a neat routine," I said. "Up to a point. After you fingered me, if I didn't buy the act, Blackie would plug me—with a dope dart. If I did—I'd be so grateful, I'd come here."

"As indeed you have." My little man looked less diffident now, more relaxed, less eager to please. A lot less eager to please.

"Your mistake," I said, "was in trying to work too many angles at once. What did you have in mind for Blackie—after?"

His face went stiff. "After—what?"

"Whatever it was, it wouldn't have worked," I said. "He was onto you, too."

". . . too?" He leaned forward as if puzzled and made a nice hip draw and showed me a strange-looking little gun, all shiny rods and levers.

"You will now tell me all about yourself, Mr. Ravel—or whatever you choose to call yourself."

"Wrong again—Karg," I said.

For an instant it didn't register. Then his fingers twitched and the gun made a spitting sound and needles showered off my chest. I let him fire the full magazine. Then I lifted the pistol I had palmed while he was arranging the chairs, and shot him under the left eye.

He settled in his chair. His head was bent back over his left shoulder as if he were admiring the water spots on the ceiling. His little pudgy hands opened and closed a couple of times. He leaned sideways quite slowly and hit the floor like two hundred pounds of heavy machinery.

Which he was, of course.

◇ **3** ◇

I went over to the door and listened for sounds that would indicate that someone had heard the shots and felt curious about them. Apparently nobody had. It was that kind of neighborhood.

I laid the Karg out on its back and cut the seal on its reel compartment, lifted out the tape it had been operating on.

It had been suspected back at Central that something outside the usual pattern had been going on back here in the Old Era theater of operations. But not even the Master Timecaster had suspected collusion between Second and Third Era operatives. The tape might be the key the Nexx planners were looking for.

But I still had my professional responsibilities. I suppressed the impulse to cut-and-run and got on with the business at hand.

The tape was almost spent, meaning the Karg's mission had been almost completed. Well, true enough, but not in quite the way that had been intended. I tucked the reel away in the zip-down pocket inside my shirt and checked the robot's pockets—all empty—then stripped it and looked for the ID data, found it printed on the left sole.

It took me twenty minutes to go over the room. I found a brainreader focused on the rocker from one of the dead bulbs in the ceiling light. The Karg had gone to a lot of trouble to make sure he cleaned me before disposing of the remains. I recorded my scan to four-point detail, fussed around a few minutes longer rechecking what I'd already checked, but I was just stalling. I'd done what I'd come here to do. The sequence of events had gone off more or less as planned back at Nexx Central; decoying the Karg into a lonely place for disposal wrapped up the operation. It was time to report in and debrief and get on with the business of remaking the cosmos. I pushed his destruct button, switched off the light, and left the room.

Back down in the street a big square car went by, making a lot of noise in the silence, but no bullets squirted from it. I was almost disappointed. But what the hell: the job was over. My stay here had been nice, but so had a lot of other times and places. This job was no different from any other. I thought about Lisa, waiting for me back at the little house we'd rented six weeks ago, after our four-day honeymoon at Niagara. She'd be getting anxious about now, trying to keep the dinner hot, and wondering what was keeping me. . . .

"Forget it," I told myself out loud. "Just get your skull under the cepher and wipe the whole thing, like you always do. You may ache a little for a while, but you won't know why. It's just another hazard of the profession."

I checked my locator and started east, downslope. My game of cat and terrier with the Karg had covered several square miles of the city of Buffalo,

New York, T.F. date, 1936. A quick review of my movements from the time of my arrival at the locus told me that I was about a mile and a half from the pickup area, thirty minutes' walk. I put my thoughts out of gear and did it in twenty-five. I was at the edge of a small park when the gauges said I was within the acceptable point/point range for a transfer back to my Timecast station. A curving path led past a bench and a thick clump of juniper. I stepped into deep shadow—just in case unseen eyes were on me—and tapped out the recall code with my tongue against the trick molars set in my lower jaw; there was a momentary pause before I felt the pickup field impinge on me, then the silent impact of temporal implosion made the ground jump under my feet——

And I was squinting against the dazzling sunlight glaring on Dinosaur Beach.

◊ **4** ◊

Dinosaur Beach had been so named because a troop of small allosaur-like reptiles had been scurrying along it when the first siting party had fixed in there. That had been sixty years ago, Nexx Subjective, only a few months after the decision to inplement Project Timesweep.

The idea wasn't without logic. The First Era of time travel had closely resembled the dawn of the space age in some ways—notably, in the trail of rubbish it left behind. In the case of the space garbage, it had taken half a dozen major collisions to convince the early space authorities of the need to sweep circumterrestrial space clean of fifty years' debris in the form of spent rocket casings, defunct telemetry gear, and derelict relay satellites long lost track of. In the process they'd turned up a surprising number of odds and ends, including lumps of meteoric rock and iron, chondrites of clearly earthly origin, possibly volcanic, the mummified body of an astronaut lost on an early space walk, and a number of artifacts that the authorities of the day had scratched their heads over and

17

finally written off as the equivalent of empty beer cans tossed out by visitors from out-system.

That was long before the days of Timecasting, of course.

The Timesweep program was a close parallel to the space sweep. The Old Era temporal experimenters had littered the timeways with everything from early one-way timecans to observation stations, dead bodies, abandoned instruments, weapons and equipment of all sorts, including an automatic mining setup established under the Antarctic icecap which caused headaches at the time of the Big Melt.

Then the three hundred years of the Last Peace put an end to that; and when temporal transfer was rediscovered in early New Era times, the lesson had been heeded. Rigid rules were enforced from the beginning of the Second Program, forbidding all the mistakes that had been made by the First Program pioneers.

Which meant that the Second Program had to invent its own disasters—which it had, in full measure. Thus the Kargs.

Karg: a corruption of "cargo," referring to the legal decision as to the status of the machine-men in the great Transport Accommodation Riots of the mid-Twenty-eighth Century.

Kargs, lifeless machines, sent back from the Third Era in the second great Timesweep attempt, designed to correct not only the carnage irresponsibly strewn across the centuries by the Old Era temporal explorers, but to eliminate the even more disastrous effects of the Second Program Enforcers.

The Third Era had recognized the impossibility of correcting the effects of human interference with more human interference. Machines which registered neutral on the life-balance scales could do what men could not do: could manipulate affairs without disturbing the delicate and poorly understood equations of vital equilibrium, to restore the integrity of the Temporal Core.

Or so they thought. After the Great Collapse and the long night that followed, Nexx Central had arisen to control the Fourth Era. The Nexx Timecasters saw clearly that the tamperings of prior eras were all part of a grand patten of confusion; that any effort to manipulate reality via temporal policing was doomed only to further weaken the temporal fabric.

When you patch time, you poke holes in it; and patching the patches makes more holes, requiring still larger patches. It's a geometric progression that soon gets out of hand; each successive salvage job sends out waves of entropic dislocation that mingle with, reinforce, and complicate the earlier waves—and no amount of paddling the surface of a roiled pond is going to restore it to a mirror surface.

The only solution, Nexx Central realized, was to remove the first causes of the original dislocations. In the beginning, of course, the disturbances set up by Old Era travelers were mere random violations of the fabric of time, created as casually and as carelessly as footprints in the jungle. Later, when it had dawned on them that every movement of a grain of sand had repercussions that went spreading down the ages, they had become careful. Rules had been made, and even enforced from time to time. When the first absolute prohibition of time meddling came along, it was already far too late. Subsequent eras faced the fact that picnics in the Paleozoic might be fun, but exacted a heavy price in the form of temporal discontinuities, aborted entropy lines, and probability anomalies. Of course, Nexx, arising as it did from this adulterated past, owed its existence to it; careful tailoring was required to undo just enough damage to restore vitality to selected lines while not eliminating the eliminator. Superior minds had to be selected and trained to handle the task.

Thus, my job as a Nexx field agent: to cancel out the efforts of all of them—good and bad, constructive or destructive; to allow the wounds in time to heal, for the great stem of life to grow strong again.

It was a worthy profession, worth all it cost. Or so the rule book said.

I started off along the shore, keeping to the damp sand where the going was easier, skirting the small tidal pools and the curving arcs of sea scum left by the retreating tide.

The sea in this era—some sixty-five million years B.C.—was South-Sea-island blue, stretching wide and placid to the horizon. There were no sails, no smudges of smoke, no beer cans washing in the tide. But the long swells coming in off the Eastern Ocean—which would one day become the Atlantic—crashed on the white sand with the same familiar *carrump—whoosh!* that I had known in a dozen eras. It was a comforting sound. It said that after all, the doings of the little creatures that scuttled on her shores were nothing much in the life of Mother Ocean, age five billion and not yet in her prime.

The station was a quarter of a mile along the beach, just beyond the low headland that jutted out into the surf; a small, low, gray-white structure perched on the sand above the high-tide line, surrounded by tree ferns and club mosses, both for decoration and to render the installation as inconspicuous as possible, on the theory that if the wildlife were either attracted or repelled by a strange element in their habitat, uncharted U-lines might be introduced into the probability matrix that would render a thousand years of painstaking—and painful—temporal mapping invalid.

In a few minutes I'd be making my report to Nel Jard, the Chief Timecaster. He'd listen, ask a few questions, punch his notes into the Masterplot and pour me a drink. Then a quick and efficient session under the memory-editor to erase any potentially disquieting recollections arising from my tour of duty in the Twentieth Century—such as Lisa. After that, a few days of lounging around the station with other between-jobs personnel, until a new assignment came up—having no visible connection with the last one. I'd never learn just why the Karg had been placed where it was, what sort of deal it had made with the Third Era Enforcer—the man in black—what part the whole thing played in the larger pattern of the Nexx grand strategy.

And probably that was just as well. The panorama of time was too broad, the warp and the woof of its weaving too complex for any one brain to comprehend. Better to leave the mind free to focus on the details of the situation at hand, rather than diffuse it along the thousand dead-end trails that were the life of a Timecast Agent. *But Lisa, Lisa . . .*

I put the thought of her out of my mind—or tried to—and concentrated on immediate physical sensations: the hot, heavy air, the buzzing insects, the sand that slipped under my feet, the sweat trickling down my temples and between my shoulder blades. Not that those things were any fun in themselves. But in a few minutes there'd be cool clean air and soft music, a stimbath, a hot meal, a nap on a real air couch. . . .

A couple of off-duty agents, bright-eyed, efficient, came out to meet me as I came across the slope of sand to the edge of the lawn, through the open gate and in under the shade of the protopalms. They were strangers to me, but they greeted me in the casually friendly way that you develop in a lifetime of casual friendships. They asked me the routine questions about whether I had had a rough one, and I gave them the routine answers.

Inside the station the air was just as cool and clean as I'd remembered—and as sterile. The stimbath was nice—but I kept thinking of the iron-stained bathtub back home. The meal afterward was a gourmet's delight: reptile steak smothered in giant mushrooms and garnished with prawns, a salad of club-moss hearts, a hot-and-cold dessert made by a barrier-layer technique that wouldn't be perfected for another sixty-five million years but didn't compare with Lisa's lemon ice-box pie with graham-cracker crust. And the air couch was nice, but not half as nice as the hard old bed with the brass frame in the breathlessly hot room with the oak floor and the starched curtains, and Lisa curled close to me. . . .

Jard let me sleep it out before the debriefing. He was a small, harassed-looking man in his mid-fifties, with an expression that said he had seen it all and hadn't been much impressed. He gave me his tired smile and listened to what I had to say, looking out the window at the same view he'd been looking at every day for five years. He liked it that I'd gotten the tape; Kargs usually managed to destruct when cornered; my slug in the emergency computing center had prevented it this time: thus the elaborate play to get him in position with his suspicions lulled. It had all been very cleverly planned and executed, and now I was tired of it, tired of the role I'd been playing, tired of the whole damned thing.

But that was just a temporary post-mission letdown. As soon as I'd had my brain scrubbed, and had rested a few days and cleared my mind of those annoying wisps of nostalgic thought, I'd be raring to go again.

Or so I hoped. Why not? I always had in the past.

Jard asked me to hold the memory-wipe until he'd had an opportunity to go through the tape in depth. I started to protest, but some vague idea of not sounding like a whiner stopped me.

I spent the rest of the day mooching around the station, thinking about Lisa.

It was a simple case of compulsive transference, or neurotic sublimation, I knew that. At least I knew the words. But every train of thought led back to her. If I tasted a daka-fruit—extinct since the Jurassic—I thought *Lisa would like this*, and I'd imagine her expression if I brought a couple home in a brown paper sack from the IGA store at the corner, pictured her peeling them and making a fruit salad with grated coconut and blanched almonds. . . .

There was a beach party that evening, down on the wide, white sand where it curved out in a long spit to embrace a shallow lagoon, where every now and then something made a splash that was too big to be a fish. Cycads grew on the point of land and on the sand bar that was busy growing into a key. They looked like beer barrels with flowers on their sides and palm fronds sticking out of their tops. There were a few unfinished-looking pines and the usual scattering of big ferns and clumps of moss that were trying to be trees. There weren't many bothersome insects; just big, blundery ones, and the small darting batlike reptiles were keeping them under control.

I sat on the sand and watched my compatriots: strong, healthy, handsome men and women, swimming in the surf inside the sonic screen set up to discourage the ichthyosaurs, chasing each other up and down the sand—and catching each other—while the guards posted in the pits at each end of the beach watched for wandering maneaters. We built a big fire—of driftwood fetched in from a locus a few million years downstream. We sang songs from a dozen eras, ate our roast baby stegosaurian, and drank white wine imported from eighteenth-century France, and felt like the lords of creation. And I thought about Lisa.

I had trouble sleeping that night. My appointment with the cepher was scheduled for 8:00 A.M. I was up before six. I ate a light breakfast and went for a walk on the beach to enjoy a few last thoughts of Lisa and wonder if somehow in our wisdom we had missed the point somewhere. It wasn't the kind of question that had an answer, but it kept my mind occupied while I put a mile or two between me and the station. I sat for half an hour and looked at the sea and wondered what I'd do if something large and hungry stalked out of the herbage behind me. I didn't know; I didn't even much care.

A *bad train of thought, Ravel,* I told myself. *Time to get back and tidy up your mind, before you get carried away and start thinking about how easy it would be to step into the transfer booth and drop yourself back into 1936 a block from the house, ten minutes after you left. . . .*

I had gotten that far in my ruminations when I heard the shots.

It's a curious thing how in moments of stress, the mind jumps to the inconsequential. I was running, without having consciously started, sending up a spatter of spray as I dashed through the tongue of a wave that slid across in my path; and I was thinking: *I won't be stepping into that cooled air and antiseptic music again; no hot meal, no stimbath, no nap on a real air couch. . . . And no Lisa, never again Lisa . . .*

I cut up across the soft sand-drift of the point, slipping and sliding as I ploughed my way upslope, crashed through a screen of palmetto at the crest, and was looking down at the station.

I don't know what I expected to see; the detonations I had heard were as much like Old Era hardshots as anything in my experience. What I saw was a pair of bulky, gray-brown machines, track-driven, obviously armored, in the fifty-ton size range, parked on the sand a few hundred yards from the station. No smoking gun muzzles were visible, but the chunk missing from the corner of the building was adequate testimony that guns were present, even without the *rackety-boom!* and the spurt of fire that came from the featureless curve of the prow of the nearer machine. The other was in trouble. One track was mangled, and smoke was leaking from a variety of places on its surface. It gave a little hop and almost invisible fire jetted from the same spots. I dropped flat in time to get the shock wave against my ribs: a kick from a buried giant.

I came up at a dead run, spitting sand and not thinking too clearly, but absolutely, unconditionally convinced that whatever was going on down there, the only Timecast booth this side of the Pleistocene was inside the station, and the nearer I got to it before they got me, the happier I'd die.

But no one was paying any attention to me and my aspirations. The still-functional warcar—Third Era, the data processor between my ears told me inconsequentially—was coming on, firing as it came. Jard must have succeeded in erecting at least a partial screen; rainbow light flared and darted coronalike over the station with each shot. But the defenses had been designed to ward off blundering brontosaurians, not tactical implosives. It wouldn't be long. . . .

I aborted that thought and put my head down and sprinted. Fire ran across the ground in front of me and winked out; the blast sent me skittering like a paper cutout in a brisk wind. I rolled, with some half-baked idea of evading any random shots somebody might be tossing my way, and came to my feet ten of the widest yards anybody ever crossed from that welcoming hole gaping in the east wall where the espalier had been. Through it I could see what was left of a filing cabinet and the internal organs of a resage chair and some twisted and blackened rags of metal that had been restful tan wall panels; but none of it seemed to get any closer. I was running with all I had, through foot-deep glue, while hell came to a head and burst around me.

And then I was going through in a long graceful dive that fetched up against an oversized anvil someone had carelessly left lying around the place. . . .

I came drifting back out of a thick fog full of little bright lights and bellowing monsters and looked up into the sweat-slick face of Nel Jard, Station Chief.

"Pull yourself together, man!" he was yelling. He had to yell to be heard over the continuous booming of the bombardment. "Everybody else is clear. I waited for you—knew you were back inside the field. Had to tell you. . . ." What he had to tell me was drowned out in a crash that made the earlier sound effects sound like a warm-up. Things fell around us. There was a throat-burning reek of ozone in the air, along with the scents of smoke and blood and pulverized stone and hot iron. I got my feet under me in time to see Jard disappearing through the door into the Ops room. I tottered after him, saw him punching a pattern into the board. The red emergency lights went on and the buzzer started its squawk and cut off abruptly. Jard turned and saw me.

"No!" he shouted, waving me off. "Get out, Ravel! Didn't you hear a word I told you? You've got to . . . out . . . co-ordinates——"

"I can't hear you," I shouted back, and couldn't hear my own words. Jard grabbed my arm, hustled me toward the floor-drop that led to the utility tunnel.

"I've got to shift the station to null-phase, you understand? Can't let them capture it. . . ." The door was up and I was being dumped over the edge. It was all happening too fast; bewildering. *A hell of a way to treat a sick man* . . . The impact of the floor hitting my head jarred it clear for the moment.

"Run for it," Jard was calling after me, from a million miles away. "Get as far as you can. Luck, Ravel . . ."

His voice was gone and I was on all fours, then stumbling to my feet, then running, more or less. It was what Nel wanted, and he was the boss.

Then the world blew up and sent me spinning head-over-heels into limbo, and a thousand tons of hot sand poured down on top of me and sealed me away for all eternity.

◇ 5 ◇

Well, maybe not eternity, a small voice seemed to be saying in a matter-of-fact tone.

"Close enough," I said, and got a mouthful of sand. I tried to draw a breath to spit it out and got a noseful of the same. That must have triggered some primitive instincts, because suddenly I was swimming hard with both hands and both feet, clawing upward through sand, breaking through into heat and the stink of charred plastics—and air. Dusty, smoky air, but air. I coughed and snorted and breathed some of it and looked around me.

I was lying in the utility tunnel, the walls of which were buckled and bulged as if they'd been half melted. The floor was drifted a foot deep in sand, out of which I had just dug my way. I tried to make my brain work. . . .

The tunnel led to the pump room, I knew, from which a ladder led to the surface, an arrangement designed for minimal disturbance of the local scenery. All I had to do was continue in the present direction, climb the ladder, and. . . .

I'd worry about the *and* later, I decided. I was still congratulating myself on my coolness under fire when I happened to notice that for a tunnel twelve feet under the surface, the light was awfully good. It seemed to be coming from behind me. I looked back, saw a tangle of steel, through the interstices of which brilliant sunlight was pouring in dusty bars.

After a dozen or so yards the going was easier; not so much sand and debris here. The pump-room door gave me a little trouble until I remembered to pull, not push. The equipment there was all intact, ready to pump any desired amount of clean, fresh spring water up from 120 feet down. I patted the nearest pump and got a grip on the ladder. I was still dizzy and weak, but no dizzier or weaker than a landlubber in his first sea-squall. At the top, the motor whined when I pushed the button; the lid cycled open, dumping sand and a small green lizard. I crawled out and took a short breather and turned to see what there was to see.

There was the long curve of beach, pitted now, and criss-crossed by tank-tracks, and the tongue of jungle that stretched almost to the shore along the ridge. But where the station had been, there was nothing but a smoking crater.

I lay flat on the nice warm sand and looked at the scene with gritty eyes that wept copiously in the glare of the tropical Jurassic sun and felt sweat trickle down my forehead, and down my chest inside my shirt, while images went swirling through my brain: the station, the first time I had seen it, on my first jump, all those years ago. The neat, impersonal little wardrooms that almost came to seem like home after a while, always waiting for you at the end of a tough assignment; the other agents, male and female, who came and went; the in-conversation around the tables in the dining room, the crisp cleanliness, the efficiency; even the big board in Ops that showed the minute-by-minute status of the Timesweep effort up and down the ages. But the big board wasn't there any more, or the miles of microtape records, or the potted gingko tree in the lounge: all melted down to slag. . . .

I was remembering Nel Jard, yelling to me to get out . . . and something else. He'd given me a message. Something important, something I was supposed to tell somebody, someday. An exercise in futility. I'd had my last talk with a human being. I was stranded, stranded as no other man had ever been, with the possible exception of a few other Nexx agents who had dropped off the screens in far places.

But none as far as this.

On that thought, I let my head drop and the dark curtain fall.

◇ **6** ◇

When I woke the sun was setting and I was aching in places I'd forgotten I owned. Itching, too. Oversized mosquitoes that didn't seem at all surprised to find a mammal where no mammals ought to be had settled down with a commendably philosophic attitude to take a meal where they found it. I batted the most persistent ones away and walked down to see what was to be seen. I didn't appear to have any major injuries, just plenty of small cuts and large bruises and the odd contusion here and there. I reached the edge of the pit where the station had been and looked at the ruins: a fused glass bowl a hundred yards in diameter surrounded by charred plant life. Nothing had survived—no people, no equipment. And worst of all, of course, there'd be no outjump to Nexx Central with a report of what had happened—or to any other time or place.

Someone, possibly Third Era—or someone masquerading as Third Era—had blasted the station with a thoroughness I wouldn't have believed possible. And how had it been possible for them to find the place, considering the elaborate security measures surrounding the placement of the 112 official staging stations scattered across Old Era time? As for Nexx Central, nobody knew where it was, not even the men who had built it. It floated in an achronic bubble adrift on the entropic stream, never physically existing in any one space-time locus for a finite period. Its access code was buried under twelve layers of interlocked ciphers in the main tank of the Nexxial Brain. The only way to reach it was via a jump station—and not just any jump station: it had to be the one my personal jumper field was tuned to.

Which was a half-inch layer of green glass lining a hollow in the sand.

An idea appeared like a ghastly grin.

The personal emergency jump gear installed in my body was intact. There was enough E-energy in the power coil for a jump—somewhere. I lacked a target, but that didn't mean I couldn't go. All it meant was that I wouldn't know where I'd land—if anywhere.

A lot of horror stories had circulated back at Nexx Central about what happened to people who misfired on a jump. They ranged from piecemeal reception at a dozen stations strung out across a few centuries to disembodied voices screaming to be let out. Also, there were several rules against it.

The alternative was to set up housekeeping here on the beach, with or without dinosaurs, and hope that a rescue mission arrived before I died of heat, thirst, reptiles, boredom, or old age.

It called for some thinking over.

There were a few chunks of masonry scattered among the charred stumps of club mosses; I could build a fireplace out of them, kill a lizard and broil him for dinner. . . .

The idea lacked charm, but I was reluctant to discard it out of hand. It was either that or risk my identity on an experiment that I had already been assured by experts was bound to end in disaster. After all, there was no particular hurry. I was bruised, but alive; I wouldn't starve for a few days; there was water available from the pump house. And maybe the destruction of the station had registered on somebody's telltale board somewhere; maybe at this moment a relief team in crisp field-tan was assembling to jump out to the rescue.

It was almost dark now. The stars were glittering through the gloaming, just as if disaster hadn't entered the biography of Igor Ravel, Timesweeper. The surf pounded and whooshed, indifferent to the personal problems of one erect biped who had no business being within sixty-five million years of here.

As for me, I had to go to the toilet.

It seemed a rather inconsequential thing to be doing, urinating on the magic sands of the past, while looking up at the eternal stars.

After that, I mooched around a little longer, looking for a lingering trace of the magic that had been there once. Then I dug a pit in the sand and went to sleep.

◇ **7** ◇

Dawn came, and with it the dinosaurs. I had seen them before, at a distance, usually; small, shy creatures that skittered out of sight at the first touch of the subsonic beams Jard had rigged up to discourage them. Before my time, it seemed, there had been a few incidents of big specimens wandering a little too close to the vegetable garden and having to be driven off with improvised noise-makers. They were too stupid to be dangerous, it was understood, except for the danger of getting stepped on, or accidentally grazed along with a clump of foliage.

This time there were three of them. Big ones, and no subsonics available, not even an ordinary noisemaker, except for my vocal cords.

Once, I remembered, a 'caster named Dowl, out for a swim, had been trapped on the beach by a saurian with impressive teeth which had popped out of the woods between him and the station. He'd gotten out of it with nothing worse than a case of delirium tremens; the behemoth had walked past him without a glance. He was too small a tidbit, the theory was, to interest a stomach as big as that one.

I didn't find that thought consoling.

The trio coming my way were of a previously unrecorded variety we had named the Royal Jester, because of their silly grin and the array of bright-colored decorations sprouting like baubles from the cranium. They also had legs like an oversized ostrich, a long neck, and far too many teeth.

I stayed where I was, flat on the sand, and played boulder while they stalked toward me, shimmering in the heat haze. There were two big ones and one giant, eighteen feet at the shoulder if he was an inch. As they got closer, I could smell the rank, cucumber-and-dung smell of them, see the strips and patches of reticulated purple and yellow hide scaling from their backs, hear the hiss and wheeze of their breathing. They were big machines, calling for a lot of air turnover. I busied myself with some abortive calculations involving lung capacity, O_2 requirements per pound, and intake orifice area; but I gave up when they got within a hundred feet. At this range I could hear their guts rumbling.

Big Boy scented me first. His head went up; a cold reptilian eye the color of a bucket of blood rolled my way. He snorted. He drooled—about a gallon. His mouth opened, and I saw rows of snow-white teeth, some of which waggled, loose, ready to shed. He steam-whistled and started my way. It was decision time, and I didn't linger.

I took a final breath of humid beach air, a last look at the bright, brutal view of sea and sand, the high, empty, impersonal sky, and the jolly monster shape looming up against it. Then I played the tune on the console set in my jaw.

The scene twisted, slid sideways and dissolved into the painless blow of a silent club, while I looped the loop through a universe-sized Klein bottle——

Total darkness and a roar of sound like Niagara Falls going over me in a barrel.

◊ **8** ◊

For a few seconds I lay absolutely still, taking a swift inventory of my existence. I seemed to be all present, organized pretty much as usual, aches, itches and all. The torrent of sound went on, getting no louder or softer; the blackness failed to fade. It seemed pretty clear that while I had left where I was, I hadn't arrived much of anywhere.

The rulebook said that in a case of transfer malfunction to remain immobile and await retrieval; but in this case that might take quite a while. Also, there was the datum that no one had ever lived to report a jump malfunction, which suggested that possibly the rulebook was wrong. I tried to breathe, and nothing happened. That decided me.

I got to my feet and took a step and emerged as through a curtain into silence and a strange blackish light, shot through with little points of dazzling brilliance, like what you see just before you faint from loss of blood. But before I could put my head between my knees, the dazzle faded and I was looking at the jump room of a regulation Nexx Staging Station. And I could breathe.

I did that for a few moments, then turned and looked at the curtain I had come through. It was a perfectly ordinary wall of concrete and beryl steel, to my knowledge two meters thick.

Maybe the sound I had heard was the whizzing of molecules of dense metal interpenetrating with my own hundred and eighty pounds of impure water.

That was a phenomenon I'd have to let ride until later. More pressing business called for my attention first—such as finding the station chief and reporting in on the destruction of Station Ninety-nine by surprise attack.

It took me ten minutes to check every room on operations level. Nobody was home. The same for the R and R complex. Likewise the equipment division and the power chamber.

The core sink was drawing normal power, the charge was up on the transmitter plates, the green lights were on all across the panels; but nothing was tapping the station for so much as a microerg.

Which was impossible.

The links that tied a staging station to Nexx Central and in turn monitored the activities of the personnel operating out of the station always drew at least a trickle of carrier power. They had to; as long as the system existed, a no-drain condition was impossible anywhere in normal space-time.

I didn't like the conclusion, but I reached it anyway.

Either the timesweep system no longer existed— or I was outside the range of its influence. And since its influence pervaded the entire spatial-

temporal cosmos, that didn't leave much of any-
place for me to be.

All the stations were physically identical: in
appearance, in equipment, in electronic character-
istics. In fact, considering their mass production
by the time-stutter process which distributed them
up and down the temporal contour, there's a school
of thought that holds that they *are* identical; alternate temporal aspects of the same physical matrix.
But that was theory, and my present situation was
fact. Step one was to find out where I was.

I went along the passage to the entry lock—
some of the sites are located in settings where
outside conditions were hostile to what Nexx Central thinks of as ordinary life—cycled it, and almost
stepped out.

Not quite.

The ground ended about ten feet from the
outflung entry wing. Beyond was a pearly gray
mist, swirling against an invisible barrier that prevented it from dissipating. I went forward to the
edge and lay flat and looked over. The underside
curved down and back, out of sight in the nebulos-
ity. What I could see of it was as smooth and
polished as green glass.

Like the green glass crater I'd seen back on
Dinosaur Beach.

I backed off from the edge of the world and
went back inside, to the Record Section, punched
for a tape at random. The read-out flashed on the
screen: routine data on power consumption, temporal contour fluctuations, arrivals and departures;
the daily log of the station, with the station number repeated on every frame.

Station Ninety-nine.

Just what I was afraid of.

The curving underside of the island in nowhere I was perched on would fit the glass-lined hollow back at Dinosaur Beach the way a casting fits the mold. The station hadn't been destroyed by enemy gunfire; it had been scooped out of the rock like a giant dip of pistachio and deposited here.

I was safe in port, my home station. That had been what Nel Jard had been trying to tell me. He'd waited until I was clear, then pulled a switch. Crash emergency procedure that an ordinary field man would know nothing about.

No doubt Jard had done the right thing. The enemy had been at the gates. In another few seconds the screens would have collapsed under overload. All the secrets of Nexx Timecasting would have fallen into hostile hands. Jard had to do something. Demolition was impossible. So he'd done this.

The fact that this implied a technology at a level far beyond what I understood of Nexx capabilities was a point I'd take up later, after more immediate matters were dealt with.

In the minutes I'd been there, he'd given me a message; something I was supposed to tell someone, somewhere. I hadn't heard a word he'd said, but in the excitement, he hadn't realized that. He'd hustled me on my way, counted ten, and thrown the switch. The station was gone but I was in the clear.

And then I had negated all that effort on his part by using my built-in circuitry to jump back where I wasn't supposed to be.

Null phase, the phrase popped into my mind. A theoretical notion I'd encountered in technical reading. But it seemed it was more than theory.

A place outside time and space. The point of

zero amplitude in the oscillations of the Ylem field that we called space-time.

I walked across the room, conscious of my feet hitting the floor, of the quiet whispering of the air circulator, the hum of idling equipment. Everything I could see, hear, smell, and touch seemed perfectly normal—except for what was outside.

But if this was the Dinosaur Beach station—where was the hole in the lounge wall that I'd come in by a few subjective hours earlier? Where was the debris and the smoke, and where the dead bodies and the wreckage?

The place was neat as an egg. I pulled out a tape drawer. Files all in order, no signs of hasty evacuation, enemy action, or last-minute confusion. Just no people—and nothing much in the way of a neighborhood.

It was the *Marie Celeste* syndrome with a vengeance—except that I was still aboard.

I went into the dining room; there were a couple of trays there with the remains of food still on them, fairly fresh: the only exception to the total and impersonal order in the station.

I poked the disposal button and punched out a meal of my own. It slid from the slot, steaming hot; syntho-this and pseudo-that. I thought of baked ham and corn on the cob—and Lisa waiting for me in the perfumed darkness. . . .

Damn it all—it wasn't supposed to be like this. A man went out, did his job, involved himself—and tore himself away to follow the call of duty—on the premise that the torture of memory would all be soothed away by the friendly mind-wiper. It wasn't in the contract that I should sit here in the gloaming in an empty station eating sawdust and ashes and yearning for a voice, a smile, a touch. . . .

What the hell, she was just a woman—an ephemeral being, born back in the dawn of time, living a life brief as the fitful glow of a firefly, dead and dust these millennia. . . .

But Lisa, Lisa . . .

"Enough of that," I told myself sternly, and quailed at the sound of my voice in the deserted station. *There's a simple explanation for everything,* I told myself, silently this time. *Well, maybe not simple, but an explanation.*

"Easy," I said aloud, and to hell with the echo. "The transfer process shifted the station back to an earlier temporal fix. Same station, different time. Or maybe no time at all. The math would all work out, no doubt. The fact that I wouldn't understand it is mere detail. The station exists—somewhere—and I'm in it. The question before the house is what do I do next?"

The air hung around me, as thick and silent as funeral incense. Everything seemed to be waiting for something to happen. And nothing would happen unless I made it happen.

"All right, Ravel," I said. "Don't drag your feet. You know what to do. The only thing you *can* do. The only out . . ."

I got to my feet and marched across to Ops, down the transit tunnel to the transfer booth.

It looked normal. Aside from the absence of a cheery green light to tell me that the outlink-circuits were locked on focus to Nexx Central, all was as it should be. The plates were hot, the dial readings normal.

If I stepped inside, I'd be transferred—somewhere.

Some more interesting questions suggested themselves, but I had no time to go over those. I stepped inside and the door valved shut and I was alone with my thoughts. Before I could have too many of those I reached out and tripped the Xmit button.

A soundless bomb blew me motionlessly across dimensionless space.

◇ 9 ◇

A sense of vertigo that slowly faded; the gradual impingement of sensation: heat, and pressure against my side, a hollow, almost musical soughing and groaning, a sense of lift and fall, a shimmer of light through my eyelids, as from a reflective surface in constant restless movement. I opened my eyes; sunlight was shining on water. I felt the pressure of a plank deck on which I was lying; a pressure that increased, held steady, then dwindled minutely.

I moved, and groaned at the aches that stabbed at me. I sat up.

The horizon pivoted to lie flat, dancing in the heat-ripples, sinking out of sight as a rising bulwark of worn and sunbleached wood rose to cut off my view. Above me, the masts, spars, and cordage of a sailing ship thrust up, swaying, against a lush blue sky. Hypnobriefed data popped into focus: I recognized the typical rigging of a sixteenth-century Portuguese galleass.

But not a real galleass, I knew somehow. A replica, probably from the Revival, circa A.D. 2220;

45

a fine reproduction, artfully carved and fitted and
weather-scarred, probably with a small reactor below
decks, steel armor under the near-oak hull plank-
ing, and luxury accommodations for an operator
and a dozen holiday-makers.

I became aware of background sounds; the creak
of ropes and timbers, a mutter of talk, a shout,
heavy rumblings. Something thudded on deck.
The ship heeled sharply; stinging salt spray came
over the weather rail and made me gasp. I blinked
it away and saw another ship out there, half a mile
away across the water, a heavy two-decker, with
three masts, flying a long green pennant with a
gray-white Maltese cross. Little white puffs appeared all along her side, with bright flashes at
their centers. A moment later, a row of water
spouts appeared in the sea, marching in a row
across our bows. Then the *baroom—om!* came
rolling after, like distant thunder.

My ideas underwent a sudden and drastic change.
The picture of a party of holiday-makers cruising
the Caribbean in their make-believe pirate ship
vanished like the splashes made by the cannon-
balls fired by the galleon. They were shooting real
guns, firing real ammunition, that could make a
real hole in the deck right where I was lying.

I rolled to my feet and looked aft. A knot of men
were there, grouped around a small deck gun they
seemed to be having trouble wrestling into position. They were dressed in sixteenth-century costumes, worn, soiled, and sweat-stained. One of
them was bleeding from a cut on the face. The
wound looked much too authentic to be part of a
game.

I dropped down behind a large crate lashed to
the deck, containing a live turtle with a chipped

and faded shell a yard in diameter. He looked as old and tired and unhappy as I felt.

Shouts, and something came fluttering down from aloft to slap against the deck not far from me: a tattered banner, coarse cloth, crudely dyed, sunfaded, with a device of an elongated green chicken with horns writhing on a dirty yellow background. Heraldry was never my strong suit; but I didn't need further clues to deduce that I was in the middle of a sea fight that my side seemed to be losing. The galleon was noticeably bigger now, coming across on the other tack. More smoke blossomed and there was a whistle and a crash up for'ard like an oil stove blowing up, and splinters rained down all around me. One of the men at the fantail went down gushing scarlet and thrashing like a boated carp. More yells, running feet. Somebody dashed past my hiding place, shouted something, maybe at me. I stayed put, waiting for an inspiration to come along and tell me what to do.

I got it in the form of a squat, swarthy man in bare brown feet, faded pinkish leggings, baggy breeches of a yellowish black, a broad hand-hacked leather belt supporting a cutlass that looked as if it had been hammered out of an old oil barrel. He stood over me and yelled, waving a short, thick arm. I got to my feet and he yelled again, waved aft, and dashed off that way.

He hadn't seemed very surprised to see me; and I had almost understood what he was yelling about. That fool Gonzalo had been idiot pig enough to get himself a gutful of taffrail, it seemed he'd said. My presence was urgently desired to assist in manning the four-pounder.

The damned fool, I heard myself snarling. *Dump the cannon over the side to lighten ship; our only chance is to outrun them, and even that's impossible. . . .*

Something screamed through the air like a rocket
and a length of rope came coiling at me and caught
me across the face and threw me across the deck.
Somebody jumped over me; a piece of spar the
size of my thigh slammed the deck and bounced
high over the side. The ship was heeling again,
coming around; things were sliding across the deck;
then the sails were slatting, taken aback. Wind
swept across the deck, cool and sweet. More thunder, more crashes, more yells, more running feet.
I found a sheltered spot in the scuppers, not too
fastidious now about the pinkish scum sloshing
there, and watched the mainmast lean, making
noises like pistol shots, and go crashing over the
windward side, trailing a ballooning tent of cloth
that split and settled over the stern and was pulled
over the side by the current, taking along a man or
two who were trapped under it. Things were falling from above like the aftermath of a dynamite
blast. Something dark loomed and suddenly spars
and sails were sliding across up above, and then an
impact threw me on my face and went on and on,
grinding splinters, snapping lines, tilting the
deck. . . .

I slipped and slithered, caught a rope, held on,
jammed against the side of the small cabin. The
galleon was still scraping alongside, looking enor-
mous. Men were in her rigging and lined up along
her waist ten feet above our deck, shouting and
waving fists and swords. I was looking down the
black muzzles of cannons that slipped past, staring
from dark square windows with smoke-blackened
faces grinning behind them. Grappling hooks came
down, slid and caught in the splintered decking.

Then men were leaping down, spilling over the rail, overrunning the deck. The seaman who had yelled at me ran forward and a saber swung at his head; it didn't seem like much of a blow, but he went down, very bloody, and the boarders crowded past, fanning out, yelling like demons. I hugged the deck and tried to look *hors de combat*. A big barrel-chested fellow swinging a machete with a badly bent blade came bounding my way; I rolled far enough to get a hand on my Mauser and got it up in time and put two through his broad, sweat-gleaming, hair-matted chest and kicked aside as he fell hard on the spot where I'd been lying. In the mêlée the shots hadn't been audible.

A little fellow with bare, monkeylike legs was trying to climb the foremast; someone jumped after him, caught him, pulled him back down. Someone went over the rail, alive or dead I wasn't sure. Then they were just milling around, yelling as loud as ever, but waving their cutlasses instead of hacking with them—except for the few who were lying here and there like broken toys, ignored, out of it, holding their wounds together with their hands and mumbling the final Hail Mary's.

Then I saw the Karg.

- - - - - - - - - - - - - - - -
- - - - - - - - - - the - - - - - - . - -
- - - - - - - - - - - - - - - - - - -
- - - - - - - - - - - - - - - - - -

◇ **10** ◇

There was no doubt of his identity. To the un-
trained eye a Class-One Karg—the only kind ever
used in Timesweep work—was indistinguishable
from any other citizen. But my eye wasn't un-
trained. Besides which, I knew him personally.

He was the same Karg I'd left in the hotel room
back in Buffalo, defunct, with a soft-nosed slug in
the left zygomatic arch.

Now here he was, pre-Buffalo, with no hole in
his head, climbing down onto the deck as neat and
cool as if it had all been in fun. From the draggled
gold lace on his cuffs and the tarnished brass hilt
on his sword, I gathered that he was a person of
importance among the victors. Possibly the captain; or maybe officer in charge of the marines.
They were listening to him, falling into ragged
ranks, quieting down.

The next step would be the telling off of details
for a systematic looting of the ship, with a side-
order of mercy killing for anyone unlucky enough
to have survived the assault.

From what I remembered of conditions in the holds of Spanish ships of the time, a fast demise was far preferable to the long voyage home, with the galleys at the end of it. I was just beginning to form a hopeless plan for creeping out of sight and waiting for something that looked like an opportunity to turn up, when the door I was lying against opened. Tried to open, that is. I was blocking it, so that it moved about two inches and jammed tight. Somebody inside gave it a hearty shove and started through. I saw a booted leg and an arm in a blue sleeve with gold buttons. He got that far and stuck. Something on his belt seemed to be caught in the door hardware. The Karg's head had turned at the first sound. He stared for a long, long time that was probably less than a second, then whipped up a handsome pearl-mounted wheel-lock pistol, raised it deliberately, aimed——

The explosion was like a bomb; flame gouted and smoke gushed. I heard the slug hit; a solid, meaty smack, like a well-hit ball hitting the fielder's glove. The fellow in the door lurched, thrashed, plunged through and went down hard on his face. He jerked a couple of times as if someone was jabbing him with a sharp stick, and then lay very still.

The Karg turned back to his men and rapped out an order. The boys muttered and shuffled, and shot disappointed looks around the deck, and then started for the side.

No search, no loot, just the fast skiddoo.

It was as if the Karg had accomplished what he had come for.

In five minutes the last of the boarders were back aboard their own ship. The Karg stood near the stern, patient as only a machine can be. He

looked around, then came toward me. I lay very
still indeed and tried to look as dead as possible.

He stepped over me and the real corpse and
went into the cabin. I heard faint sounds, the kind
somebody makes going through drawers and peeking under the rug. Then he came out. I heard his
footsteps going away, and opened an eye.

He was by the weather rail, calmly stripping the
safety foil from a thermex bomb. It gave its pre-
liminary hiss and he dropped it through the open
hatch at his feet as casually as someone dropping
an olive in a martini.

He walked coolly across the deck, stepped up,
grabbed a line, and scrambled with commendable
agility back to his own deck. I heard him—or
someone—yell a command. Sounds of sudden activity; sails quivered and moved; men appeared,
swarming up the ratlines. The galleon's spars shifted,
withdrew with much creaking and tearing of the
defeated galleass's rigging. The high side of the
Spanish ship drew away; sails filled with dull
*boom!*s. Quite suddenly I was alone, watching the
ship dwindle as it receded downwind under full
sail.

Just then the thermex let go with a vicious
choof! belowdecks. Smoke billowed from the hatch,
with tongues of pale flame in close pursuit. I got a
pair of legs under me and wobbled to the opening,
had to turn my eyes from the sunbright holocaust
raging below. The tub might have steel walls, but
in 5000° heat they'd burn like dry timber.

I stood where I was for a few valuable seconds,
trying to put it together in some way that made
some variety of sense, while the fire sputtered and
crackled and the deck wallowed, and the shadow
of the stump of the mainmast swung slow arcs on

the deck, like a finger wagging at the man the Karg had shot.

He lay on his face, with a lot of soggy lace in a crimson puddle under his throat. One hand was under him, the other outflung. A gun lay a yard from the empty hand.

I took three steps and stooped and picked up the gun. It was a .01 microjet of Nexx manufacture, with a grip that fitted my hand perfectly.

It ought to. It was my gun. I looked at the hand it had fallen from. It looked like my hand. I didn't like doing it, but I turned the body over and looked at the face.

It was my face.

◊ **11** ◊

The standard post-mission conditioning that had wiped the whole sequence from my memory broke. I remembered it now: Time, about ten years earlier, N.S.; or the year 1578, local. Place, the Caribbean, about fifty miles southwest of St. Thomas. It had been a cruise in search of the Karg-operated ship which had been operating in New Spanish waters; I recalled the contact, the chase, the fight across the decks while I waited inside the cabin for the opportunity for the single well-placed shot that would eliminate the source of the interference. It was one of my first assignments, long ago completed, filed in the master tape, a part of Timesweep history.

But not anymore. The case was reopened on the submission of new evidence. I was doubled back on my own timetrack.

The fact that this was a violation of every natural law governing time travel was only a minor aspect of the situation, grossly outweighed by this evidence that the past that Nexx Central had painfully rebuilt to eliminate the disastrous effects of Old Era time meddling was coming unstuck.

And if one piece of the new mosaic that was being so carefully assembled was coming unglued—then everything that had been built on it was likewise on the skids, ready to slide down and let the whole complex and artificial structure collapse in a heap of temporal rubble that neither Nexx Central nor anyone else would be able to salvage.

With the proper lever, you can move worlds; but you need a solid place to stand. That had been Nexx Central's job for the past six decades: to construct a platform in the remote pre-Era on which all the later structure would be built.

And it looked as though it had failed—because of me.

I remembered the way it had gone the first time: waiting my moment, thrusting the door open, planting my feet, taking aim, firing three shots into the android's thoracic cavity before he was aware that a new factor had entered the equation. He had fallen; his men had yelled in rage and charged, and my repellor field had held them off until they panicked at the invisible barrier and fled back to their galleon, cast off, and made sail before the wind, back into the obscurity of unrecorded history; while I had brought the galleass—a specially equipped Nexx operations unit in disguise—to the bulk transfer point at Locus Q-637, from which it had been transmitted back to storage at the Nexx holding station.

But none of that had happened.

I had blocked the door, preventing the *other* me from completing his assignment, thus invalidating a whole segment of the rebuilt time-map and casting the whole grand strategy of Nexx operations into chaos. The Karg had gone his way, unharmed; and I was lying on the deck, very dead indeed from a brass ball through the throat.

And also I was standing on the deck looking down at my corpse, slowly realizing the magnitude of the trap I had blundered into.

A Nexx agent is a hard man to dispose of: hard to kill, hard to immobilize, because he's protected by all the devices of a rather advanced science.

But if he can be marooned in the closed loop of an unrealized alternate reality—a pseudo-reality from which there can be no outlet to a future which doesn't exist—then he's out of action forever.

Even if I could go on living—a doubtful proposition in view of the fire curling the deck planks at the moment—there'd be no escape, ever; my personal jump field was discharged; it wouldn't take me anywhere. And there'd be no trace on any recording instrument to show where I'd gone; when I'd jumped from the phantom station, I'd punched in no destination. The other me had now been killed in the line of duty, during the vulnerable second when his shield was open to allow him to fire the executioner's shot. His trace would have dropped from the boards; scratch one inefficient field man, who'd been so careless as to get himself killed.

And scratch his double, who'd poked his nose in where it had no business being.

My mind circled the situation, looking for an out. I didn't like what I found, but I liked it better than roasting alive or drowning in the tepid sea.

My personal jump mechanism was built into me, tuned to me, though unfocused at the receiving end. It would be useless until I'd had a recharge at base. But its duplicate was built into the corpse lying at my feet. The circuitry of the jump device—from antennae to powerpack—consisted largely of the nervous system of the owner.

It took only five minutes without oxygen for irreversible brain damage to occur. At least four had already passed, but the dead man's circuitry should be operable. Just what it might be focused on now—considering the drastic realignment of the casual sequence—was an open question. It would depend to a degree on what had been on the corpse's mind at the moment of death.

The deck was getting hot enough to burn my feet through my soles. There was lots of smoke. The fire roared like a cataract in flood season.

I squatted beside the dead version of myself. The corpse's jaws were in a half-open position. I got a finger inside and tried out my recall code on the molar installation, feeling the blast of heat as flames gouted from the open hatch at my back.

A giant clapped his hands together, with me in the middle.

◇ **12** ◇

It was dark and I was falling; I just had time to realize the fact and claw for nonexistent support before I hit water: hot, stinking, clogged with filth, thick as pea soup; I went under and came up blowing and gagging. I was drowning in slime: I floundered, tried to swim, arrived at an uneasy equilibrium in which I lay out flat, head raised clear of the surface, paddling just enough to keep my nostrils clear, while goo ran down in my eyes.

The smell could have been sliced and sold for linoleum. I spat and coughed and sploshed and my hand scraped a surface that sloped gently up under me. My knees bumped and I was crouched on all fours, snorting and trying without much luck to squeeze the muck from my eyes. I tried to crawl forward and slipped and slid backward and almost dunked my head again.

I did it more carefully the next time: eased forward, with most of my weight supported by the semiliquid goo, and felt over the shore. It wasn't like any shore I had ever encountered before; hard-surfaced, planar, as smooth as a toilet bowl, curving gently upward. I groped my way along sideways, slipping, splashing, suffocating in the raw-sewage reek. Something spongy and rotting came apart under my hands. I tried again to crawl forward, made a yard and slid back two.

I was getting tired. There was nothing to hold onto. I had to rest. But if I rested, I sank. I thought about sliding down under that glutinous surface and trying to breathe and getting a lungful of whatever it was I was floundering in, and dying there and turning to something as black and corrupt as what I was buried in——

It was a terrible thought. I opened my mouth and yelled.

And somebody answered.

"You down there! Stop kicking around! I'm throwing you a line!"

It was a female voice, not to say feminine, coming from above me somewhere. It sounded sweeter than a choir of massed angels. I tried to call out a cheery and insouciant reply, managed a croak. A beam of white light speared down at me from a point thirty feet above and fifty feet away. It hunted across the bubbly black surface and glared in my eyes.

"Lie still!" the voice commanded. The light went away, bobbled around, came back. Something came whistling down and slapped into the muck a few feet away. I floundered and groped, encountered a half-inch rope slick with the same stuff I was slick with.

"There's a loop at the end. Put your foot in it. I'll haul you up."

The rope slid through my hands; I scrabbled, felt the knot, got another dipping trying to hook a foot in it, settled for a two-handed grip. The rope surged, pulling me clear of the stew and up the slope. I held on and rode. The surface under me curved up and up. Progress was slowed. Another yard. Another. Half a yard. A foot. I was at an angle of about thirty degrees now, pressed tight against the slope. Another surge and I heard the rope rasping above. An edge raked my forearm. I grabbed, almost lost the rope, was dragged up the final foot and got a knee over the edge and crawled forward across loose sand and went down on my face and out.

◇ **13** ◇

Sun in my eyes. Forgot to pull down the shades. Lumpy mattress. Too hot. Sand in the bed. Itches; aches. . . .

I unglued an eyelid and looked at white sand that undulated down to the shore of a brassy sea. A lead-colored sky, but bright for all that; a gray wave that slid in and *crump!*ed on the beach. No birds, no sails, no kids with buckets, no bathing beauties. Just me and the eternal sea.

It was a view I knew all too well. I was back on Dinosaur Beach, and it was early in the morning, and I hurt all over.

Things cracked and fell away as I sat up, using a couple of broken arms that happened to be handy. There was gray mud caked on my trousers, gluing them to my legs; gray mud covered my shoes. I bent my knee and almost yelped at the pain. The cloth cracked and mud broke and crumbled. I was coated in the stuff like a shrimp in batter. It was on my face, too. I scraped at it, breaking off shells, prying it loose from my sideburns, spitting it. It was in my eyes; I fingered them, making matters worse.

"You're awake, I see," a crisp voice said from somewhere behind me. I dug mud from my ear and could hear her feet squeaking in the sand. The sound of something being dumped nearby.

"Don't claw at your eyes," she said sharply. "You'd better go down to the water and wash yourself clean."

I grunted and got both knees and both hands firmly planted and stood up. A firm hand took my right arm just above the elbow—rather gingerly, I thought—and urged me forward. I walked, stumbling, through the loose sand. The sun burned against my eyelids; the sound of surf grew louder. I crossed firm sand that sloped down, and then warm water was swirling around my ankles. She let go and I took a few more steps and sank down in the water and let it wash over me.

The dry mud turned back to slime, releasing a sulphurous stench. I sluiced water over my head, scoured my scalp more or less clean, put my face in the water and scrubbed at it, and could see again.

I pulled my shirt off, mud-heavy, sodden, swished it back and forth, trailing a dark cloud in the murky-pale green. Various small cuts and one larger one across my forearm were leaking pink. My knuckles were raw. The salt water burned like acid. I noticed that the back of my shirt was gone, leaving a charred edge. The sky had turned a metallic black, filled with small whirly lights. . . .

Splashing sounds behind me. Hands on me, pulling me up. I seemed to have been drowning without knowing it. I coughed and retched while she half-dragged me back up through the surf onto the beach. My legs weren't working very well. They got tangled up and I went down, and rested like that for a minute on all fours, shaking my head to drive away the high, whining noise that seemed to be coming from a spot deep between my ears.

"I didn't realize . . . you're hurt. Your back . . . burns . . . what happened to you?" Her voice came from far away, swelling and fading.

"The boy stood on the burning deck," I said airily, and heard it come out slurred gibberish. I could see a pair of trim female shins in fitted leather boots, a nice thigh under gray whipcord, a pistol belt, a white shirt that had probably been crisp once. I grunted again, just to let her know I was still in there pitching, and got my feet under me and stood, with her hauling on my arm.

". . . left you outside all night . . . first aid . . . you walk . . . ? . . . little way . . ." Some of the drill-sergeant snap was gone from the voice. It sounded almost familiar. I turned and blinked against the sun and looked into her face, which was frowning at me in an expression of deep concern, and felt my heart stop dead for a full beat.

It was Lisa.

◇ **14** ◇

I croaked something and grabbed at her; she fended me off and looked stern, like a night nurse not liking her job but doing it anyway.

"Lisa—how did you get here?" I got the words out somehow.

"My name isn't Lisa—and I got here in the same way I suspect you did." She was walking me toward a small field tent, regulation issue, that was pitched higher up on the beach, under the shade of the club mosses. She gave me another no-nonsense look. "You *are* a field man, I suppose?" Her eyes were taking in what was left of my clothes. She sucked in air between her teeth. "You look as if you'd been in an air raid," she said, almost accusingly.

"Ground-armor attack and a sea chase," I said. "No air raid. What are you *doing* here, Lisa? How . . ."

"I'm Mellia Gayl," she cut in. "Don't go delirious on me now. I've got enough on my hands without that."

"Lisa, don't you know me? Don't you recognize me?"

"I never saw you before in my life, mister." She ducked her head and thrust me through the tent fly, into coolness and amber light.

"Get those clothes off," she ordered. I wanted to assert my masculine prerogative of undressing myself, but somehow it was just a little more than I could manage. I leaned against her and slid down sideways and had my pants dragged down over my ankles. She pulled my shoes off, and my socks. I managed the wet shorts myself. I was shivering and burning up. I was a little boy and mama was putting me to bed. I felt cool softness under me and rolled over on my face, away from the remote fire at my back, and let it all fade away into a soft, embracing darkness.

◇ **15** ◇

"I'm sorry about leaving you unattended all last night," Lisa, or Mellia Gayl, said. "But of course I didn't know you were hurt—and——"

"And I was out cold and too heavy to carry, even if I'd smelled better," I filled in. "Forget it. No harm done."

It had been rather pleasant, waking up in a clean bed, in an air-conditioned tent, neatly bandaged and doped to the hairline, feeling no pain, just a nice warm glow of well-being, and a pleasant numbness in the extremities.

But Lisa still insisted she didn't know me.

I watched her face as she fiddled with the dressings she'd put on my various contusions, as she spooned soup into me. There wasn't the slightest shadow of a doubt. She was Lisa.

But somehow not quite the Lisa I'd fallen in love with.

This Lisa—Mellia Gayl—was crisp, efficient, cool, unemotional. Her face was minutely thinner, her figure minutely more mature. It was Lisa, but a Lisa older by several years than the wife I had abandoned only subjective hours ago. A Lisa who had never known me. There were implications in that I wasn't ready to think about. Not yet.

"They're full of surprises, the boys back at Central," I said. "Imagine Lisa—my sweet young bride—being a Timesweep plant. Hard to picture. Took me completely. I thought I met her by accident. All part of the plan. They could have told me. Some actress . . ."

"You're tiring yourself out," Mellia said coolly. "Don't try to talk. You've lost a lot of blood and plasma. Save your strength for recuperating."

"Otherwise you're stuck with an invalid or a corpse, eh, kid?" I thought, but the spoon went into my mouth in time to keep me from saying it.

"I heard the splash," she was saying. "I knew something big was thrashing around down there. I thought a small reptile had blundered into it. It's a regular trap. They fall in and can't get out again." As she spoke, her voice sounded younger, more vulnerable.

"But you came and had a look anyway," I said. "Animal lover."

"I was glad when you shouted," she blurted, as if it was a shameful admission. "I was beginning to wonder . . . to think——"

"And you still haven't told me how you happened to be waiting here to welcome me with hot soup and cold glances," I said.

She tightened up her mouth but it was still a mouth that was made for kisses.

"I'd finished up my assignment and jumped back to station," she said flatly. "But the station wasn't here. Just a hole in the ground full of mud and bones. I didn't know what to think. My first impulse was to jump out again, but I knew that

would be the wrong thing to do. There'd be no
telling where I'd end up. I decided my best course
would be to sit tight and wait for a retrieval. So
. . . here I am."

"How long?"

"About . . . three weeks."

" 'About?' "

"Twenty-four days, thirteen hours and ten minutes," she snapped, and jammed the spoon at my
teeth.

"What was your assignment?" I asked after I'd
swallowed.

"Libya. 1200 B.C."

"I never knew the ancient Libyans packed
revolvers."

"It wasn't a contact assignment, I was alone in
the desert—at an oasis, actually, at the time,
equipped for self-maintenance for a couple of weeks.
Things were a little greener there in those days.
There'd been some First Era tampering done with
an early pre-Bedouin tomb, with a complicated
chain of repercussions, tied in with the rise of
Islam much later.

"My job was to replace some key items that had
been recovered from a Second Era museum. I
managed it all right. Then I jumped back—" She
broke off and for just an instant I saw a frightened
girl trying very hard to be the tough, fearless
agent.

"You did just right, Mellia," I said. "In your
place I'd probably have panicked and tried to jump
back out. And ended up stuck in an oscillating
loop." As I said it, I realized that was the wrong
aspect of the matter to dwell on just now.

"Anyway, you waited, and here I am. Two heads,
and all that——"

"What are we going to do?" she cut in. She sounded like a frightened girl now. *Swell job of comforting you're doing, Ravel. She was fine until you came along. . . .*

"We have several courses of action," I said as briskly as I could with soup running down my chin. "Just let me . . ." I ran out of wind and drew a shaky breath. "Let me catch a few winks more and. . . ."

"Sorry . . ." she was saying. "You need your rest. Sleep; we'll talk later. . . ."

I spent three days lying around waiting for the skin on my back to regenerate, which it did nicely under the benign influence of the stuff from Mellia's field kit, and for my scrapes and cuts to seal themselves over. Twice during that time I heard shots: Mellia, discouraging the big beasties when they got too close. A crater gun at wide diffusion stung just enough to get the message through to their pea-sized brains.

On the fourth day I took a tottery stroll over to the edge of the hole Mellia had pulled me out of.

It was the pit where the station had been, of course. High tides, rain, blown sand, wandering animals had filled it halfway to the brim. The glass lining above the surface was badly weathered. It had taken time for that—lots of time.

"How long?" Mellia asked.

"Centuries, anyway. Maybe a thousand or two years."

"That means the station was never rebuilt," she said.

"At least not in this time segment. It figures; if the location was known there was no reason to go on using it."

"There's more to it than that. I've been here for

almost a month. If anyone were looking for me, they'd have pinpointed me by now."

"Not necessarily. It's a long reach, this far back."

"Don't try to be kind to me, Ravel. We're in trouble. This is more than a little temporary confusion. Things are coming apart."

I didn't like her using virtually the same wording that had popped into my mind when I'd looked at my own corpse.

"The best brains at Nexx Central are working on this," I told her. "They'll come up with the answers." It didn't sound convincing even to me.

"What was the station date when you were there last?" she asked.

"Sixty-five," I said. "Why?"

She gave me a tense little smile. "We're not exactly contemporaries. I was assigned to Dino Beach in twelve-thirty-one, local."

I let the impact of that diffuse through my brain for a few seconds, bringing no comfort. I grunted as if I'd been socked in the gut.

"Swell. That means—" I let it hang there; she knew what it meant as well as I did: that the whole attack I had seen—lived through—the consequences of which we were looking at now—was what was known to the trade as a recidivism: an aborted alternate possibility that either had never occurred or had been eliminated by Timesweep action. In Mellia's past, the Dinosaur Beach station had been functional for over eleven hundred years, minimum, after the date I'd seen it under attack. She'd jumped from it to Libya, done her job, and jumped back—to find things changed.

Changed by some action of mine.

I had no proof of that assumption, of course; but I knew. I'd handled my assignment in 1936 according to the book, wrapped up all the loose ends, scored a total victory over my Karg counterpart. I thought.

But something had gone wrong. Something I'd done—or not done—had shattered the pattern. And the result was this.

"It doesn't make sense," I said. "You jumped back to home base and found it missing—the result of something that didn't happen in your own personally experienced past. O.K. But what puts me here at the same time? The circuits I used for my jump were tuned to a point almost twelve hundred years earlier."

"Why haven't they made a pick-up on me?" she said, not really talking to me. Her voice was edging up the scale a little.

"Take it easy, girl," I said, and patted her shoulder; I knew my touching her would chill her down again. Not a nice thing to know, but useful.

"Keep your hands to yourself, Ravel," she snapped, all business again. "If you think this is some little desert island scene, you're very wrong."

"Don't get ahead of yourself," I told her. "When I make a pass at you that'll be time enough to slap me down. Don't go female on me now. We don't have time for nonsense."

She sucked in air with a sharp hiss and bottled up whatever snappy comeback she'd been about to make. Quite a girl. It was all I could do to keep from putting my arms around her and telling her it was all going to be all right. Which was a long way from what I believed.

"We can sit here and wait it out for a while longer," I said, in my best business-as-usual tone. "Or we can take action now. How do you vote?"

"What action?" It was a challenge.

"In my opinion," I said, not taking the bait, "the possible benefits of staying put are very small—statistically speaking. Still, they exist."

"Oh?" Very cool; just a little tremble of a finely molded lip that was beaded with sweat.

"This is a known locus; whatever the difficulties that caused the site to be abandoned, it's still a logical place for a search effort to check."

"That's nonsense. If it were checked and we were located the sensible thing to do—or at least the humane thing—would be to shift the pick-up back a month and take us out at the moment of our arrival. That didn't happen. Therefore it won't happen."

"Maybe you've forgotten what this Timesweep effort is all about, Miss Gayl. We're trying to knit the fabric back together, not make new holes in it. If we were spotted here, now—and the pick-up were made at a prior locus—what happens to all the tender moments we've known together? This moment right now? It never happened? No, any pick-up on us would be made at the point of initial contact, not earlier. However . . ."

"Well?"

"The possibility exists that we're occupying a closed-loop temporal segment, not a part of the main timestem."

She looked a little pale under the desert tan, but her eyes held mine firmly.

"In which case—we're marooned—permanently."

I nodded. "Which is where the alternative comes in."

"Is there . . . one?"

"Not much of one. But a possibility. Your personal jumper's still operational."

"Nonsense. I'm tuned to home on the station

fix. I'm already at the station fix. Where would I go?"

"I don't know. Maybe nowhere."

"What about you?"

I shook my head.

"I already used my reserve. Charge is gone. I'll have to wait for you to bring help back. So—I'll contain myself in patience—if you decide to try it, that is."

"But—an unfocused jump——"

"Sure—I've heard the scare stories too. But my jump wasn't so bad. I ended up in the station, remember?"

"A station in nowhere, as you described it."

"But with a transfer booth. When I used it, it pitched me back down my own timeline. As luck would have it, I ended up looking in on a previous field assignment. Maybe you'll be luckier."

"That's all that's left, isn't it? Luck."

"Better than nothing."

She stood, not looking at me; my Lisa, so hurt and so bewildered, so scared and trying not to show it, so beautiful, so desirable. I wondered if she had known—if it had been a sleeper assignment, meaning a field job in which the agent was conditioned to be unaware of his actual role, believed himself to be whatever his cover required.

"You really want me to go?" she said.

"Looks like the only way," I said. Good old iceberg Ravel, not an emotion in his body. "Unless you want to set up permanent housekeeping with me here on the beach." I gave her a nice leer to help her make her decision.

"There's another way," she said in a voice chipped out of ice. I didn't answer.

"My field will carry both of us," she said.

"Theoretically. Under, uh, certain conditions——"

"I know the conditions."

"Oh, hell, girl, we're wasting time——"

"You'd let me abandon you here before you'd . . ." She paused. ". . . meet those conditions?"

I drew a breath and tried to keep the strain out of my voice. "Not abandon. You'll be back."

"We'll go together," she said, "or not at all."

"Look, Miss Gayl, you don't have to——"

"Oh, yes, I *do* have to. Make no mistake about that, Mr. Ravel!"

She turned and walked off across the sand, looking very small and very forlorn against all that emptiness of beach and jungle.

I waited five minutes, for some obscure reason, before I followed her.

◇ **16** ◇

She was waiting for me in the tent. She had
undressed and put on a lightweight robe. She
stood beside the field bed which she had deployed
to its full forty-inch width and looked past my
shoulder. Her expression was perfectly calm, perfectly cool. I went across to her and put my hands
lightly on her ribs just above her hips. Her skin
was silk-smooth under the thin robe. She stiffened
a little. I moved my hands up until the weight of
her breasts was pressing against the heels of my
hands. I drew her closer to me; she resisted minutely, then let her weight come against me. Her
hair touched my face, soft as a cloud. I held her
close. I was having a little trouble drawing a deep
breath.

She pulled away suddenly, half turned away.

"What are you waiting for?" she said in a brittle
voice.

"Maybe it would be better to wait," I said.
"Until after dark . . ."

"Why?" she snapped. "So it would be more
romantic?"

"Maybe; something like that."

"In case you've forgotten, Mr. Ravel, this isn't romance. It's expediency."

"Speak for yourself, Mellia."

"I assure you, I am!" She turned and faced me; her face was pink, her eyes bright.

"Damn you, get on with it!" she whispered.

"Unbutton my shirt," I said, very quietly. She just looked at me.

"Do as I said, Mellia."

Her expression went uncertain, then started to firm up into a sneer.

"Cut it!" I said with plenty of snap. "This was your idea, not mine, lady. I didn't force myself on you; I'm still not. But unless you want to make the grand sacrifice in vain, you'd better get into the spirit of the thing. Physical intimacy isn't the magic ingredient—it's psychological contact, the meeting and merging and sharing of personalities as well as bodies. The sexual aspect is merely the vehicle. So unless you can nerve yourself to stop thinking of me as a rapist, you can forget the whole idea."

She closed her eyes and drew a deep breath and let it out and looked at me again. Her lashes were wet; her mouth had gone all soft and vulnerable.

"I'm . . . sorry. You're right, of course. But . . . ?"

"I know. It isn't the bridal night you dreamed of."

I took her hand; it was soft, hot, unresisting.

"Have you ever been in love, Mellia?"

Her eyes winced; just a flicker of pain. "Yes."

Lisa, Lisa . . .

"Think back; remember how it was. Pretend . . . I'm him."

Her eyes closed. How delicate the lids were, the pastel tracery of veins in the rose-petal skin. I put my hands gently on her throat, slid them down to her shoulders, under the robe. Her skin was hot, damask-smooth. I pushed the garment down and away; it dropped from her shoulders, caught on the swell of her breasts. My hands moved down, brushing the cloth aside, taking the weight of her breasts on my palms. She drew a sharp breath between her teeth; her lips parted.

She dropped her arms, shed the robe. I glanced down at the slimness of her waist, the swell of hips as she came against me.

Her hands went uncertainly to the buttons on my shirt; she leaned back, opening it, pulling out my shirttail. She unbuckled my belt, went to her knees, dragged the rest of my clothing off. I picked her up, carried her to the cot. Rounded, yielding forms moved against me; my hands explored her, trying to encompass all of her. She shivered and drew me to her; her mouth half-opened; her eyelids parted and her eyes glittered into mine an inch away; her mouth met mine hungrily. My weight went onto her; her hands were deft; her thighs pressed against mine. We moved as one.

There was no time, no space, no thought. She filled my arms, my world; beauty, pleasure, sensation, fulfillment that rose and rose to a crest of unbearable delight that crashed down like a long Pacific comber, roiling and surging, then slowing, sliding smoothly to a halt, paused, then slipped back, back, down and out and away to merge with the eternal ocean of life. . . .

◇ **17** ◇

For a long time neither of us spoke. We lay
spent in the amber light; the surf boomed and
hissed softly, the wind fluted around the tent.

Her eyes opened and looked into mine, a look
of utter candor, of questioning, perhaps of surprise. Then they closed again and she was asleep.
I rose quietly and picked up my clothes and went
outside, into the heat and the dry wind from the
dunes. A pair of small saurians were on the beach
a mile or so to the south. I dressed and went down
to the water's edge and wandered along the surf
line, watching the small life that scurried and swam
with such desperate urgency in the shallows.

The sun was low when I got back to the tent.
Mellia was busy, setting out food from the field
stores. She was wearing the robe, barefooted, her
hair unbound. She looked up at me as I came in; a
look half-wary, half-impish. She looked so young,
so achingly young. . . .

"I'll never be sorry," I said. "Even if . . ." I let
it hang there.

She looked faintly troubled. "Even if . . . what?"

"Even if we proved the theory was wrong. . . ."

She stared at me; suddenly her eyes widened.

"I forgot to—," she said. "I forgot all about it. . . ."

I felt my face curving into a silly smile. "So did I—until just now."

She put her hand over her mouth and laughed. I held her and laughed with her. Then she was crying. Her arms went around me and she clung, and sobbed, and sobbed, and I stroked her hair and made soothing noises.

◊ **18** ◊

"This time I won't forget," she whispered in my ear. *In the dark; in the perfumed darkness* . . .

"Don't count on me to remind you," I said.

"Did you—do you love her very much—your Lisa?"

"Very much."

"How did you meet her?"

"In the Public Library. We were both looking for the same book."

"And you found each other."

"I thought it was an accident." *Or a miracle* . . .

I'd only been on location for a few days, just long enough to settle into my role and discover how lonely life was back in that remote era; remote, but, for me, the present: the only reality. As was usual in a long cover assignment, my conditioning was designed to fit me completely to the environment: my identity as Jim Kelly, draftsman, occupied 99 percent of my self-identity concept. The other 1 percent, representing my awareness of my true function as a Nexx agent, was in abeyance: a faint, persistent awareness of a level of existence above the immediate details of life in ancient Buffalo; a hint of a shadowy role in great affairs.

I hadn't known consciously, when I met Lisa, wooed and won her, that I was a transient in her time, a passer-through that dark and barbaric era. When I married her, it was with the intention of living out my life with her, for better or for worse, richer or poorer, until death did us part.

But we'd been parted by something more divisive than death. As the crisis approached, the knowledge of my real role came back to me a piece at a time, as needed. The confrontation with the Karg had completed the job.

"Perhaps it *was* an accident," Mellia said. "Even if she was . . . me . . . she might have been there for another reason, having nothing to do with your job. She didn't know. . . ."

"You don't have to defend her, Mellia. I don't blame her for anything."

"I wonder what she did . . . when you didn't come back."

"If I had, I wouldn't have found her there. She'd have been gone, back to base, mission completed——"

"No! Loving you wasn't any part of her mission; it couldn't have been like that. . . ."

"She was caught, just as I was. All in a good cause, no doubt. The giant brains at Central know best——"

"Hush," she said softly, and put her lips against mine. She clung to me, holding me tight against her slim nakedness, lying in the dark. . . .

"I'm jealous of her," she whispered. "And yet—she's me."

"I want you, Mellia; every atom of me wants you. I just can't help remembering."

She made a sound that was half laugh, half sob. "You're making love to me—and thinking of her. You feel that you're betraying her—with me—" She stopped to shush me as I started to speak.

"No—don't try to explain, Ravel. You can't change it—can't help it. And you do want me . . . you want me . . . I know you want me. . . ."

And this time as we rode the passionate crest, the world exploded and tumbled us together down a long, lightless corridor and left us in darkness and in silence.

Light coalesced around us; and sound: the soft breathing of an air circulation system. We were lying naked on the bare floor in the operations room of a Nexx Timecast station.

"It's small," Mellia said. "Almost primitive." She got to her feet and padded across to the intercom panel, flipped the master.

"Anybody home?" her voice echoed along the corridors.

Nobody was. I didn't have to search the place. You could feel it in the air.

Mellia went to the Excom-board; I watched her punch in an all-stations emergency code. A light winked to show that it had been automatically taped, condensed to a one-microsecond squawk, and repeated at one-hour intervals across a million years of monitored time.

She went to the log, switched on, started scanning the last entries, her face intent in the dim glow of the screen. Watching her move gracefully, unself-consciously nude, was deeply arousing to me. I got my mind off that with an effort and went to stand beside her.

The log entry was a routine shorthand report, station-dated 9/7/66, with Dinosaur Beach's identifying key and Nel Jard's authenticating code at the end.

"That's one day prior to the day I reported back," I said. "I guess he didn't have time to file any details during the attack."

"At least he got the personnel away before. . . ." She let that ride.

"All but himself," I said.

"But—you didn't find him—or any sign of him—in the station when you were here before. . . ."

"His corpse, you mean. Nope. Maybe he used the booth. Maybe he went over the edge——"

"Ravel—" She looked at me half sternly, half appealingly.

"Yeah. I think I'll go get some clothes on. Not that I don't like playing Adam and Eve with you," I added. "I like it all too well."

We found plenty of regulation clothing neatly stacked in the drawers in the transient apartment wing. I enjoyed the cool, smooth feel of modern fabric on my skin. Getting used to starched collars and itchy wool had been one of the chief sources of discomfort in my 1936 job. That started me thinking again. . . .

I shook off the thought. Lisa—or Mellia—was standing not six feet away, pulling on a form-fitting one-piece station suit. She caught me looking at her and hesitated for an instant before zipping it up to cover her bosom, and smiled at me. I smiled back.

I went outside to take a look, knowing what I'd find: an abrupt edge ten paces from the exit, with the fog swirling around it. I yelled; no echo came back. I picked up a pebble and tossed it over the side. It fell about six feet and then slowed and drifted off as if it had lost interest in the law of gravity. I peered through the murk, looking for a rift with a view beyond it; but beyond the fog there was just more fog.

"It's . . . eerie," Mellia said beside me.

"All of that," I said. "Let's get back inside. We need sleep. Maybe when we wake up it will be gone."

She let that one pass. That night she slept in my arms. I didn't dream—except when I woke in the night and found her there.

◊ **20** ◊

At breakfast the clatter of forks against plates seemed louder than it should have been. The food was good. Nexx issue rations were designed to fill a part of the gap left in agents' lives by the absence of all human relationships and values that ordinarily made life worth living. We were dedicated souls, we field agents. We gave up homes and wives and children in the service of the concept that the human race and its destiny were worth the saving. It was a reasonable exchange. Any man ought to be able to see that.

But Lisa's face floated between me and my breakfast, the emergency I was involved in, the threat to Timesweep. Between me and Mellia.

"What are we going to do, Ravel?" Mellia said. Her expression was cool and calm now; her eyes held shielded secrets. Maybe it was the effect of the familiar official surroundings. The fun and games were over. From now on it was business.

"The first thing we need to do is take a good look at the data and see what can be deduced," I said, and felt like a pompous idiot.

"Very well; we have several observations between us that should give us some ideas of the parameters of the situation." Crisp; scientifically precise. Eyes level and steady. A good agent, Miss Gayl. *But where was the girl who had sobbed in my arms last night?*

"All right," I said. "Item: I completed a routine assignment, returned to the pickup point, sent out my callsign, and was retrieved. All normal so far." I glanced at her for agreement. She nodded curtly.

"The next day the station was attacked by Third Era Forces, or someone disguised as Third Era Forces. Aside from a rather unlikely breach of security, there's no anomaly involved there. However, *your* personal life line includes the Dino Beach station intact at a local time eleven-hundred-plus years later than the observed attack."

"Correct; and insofar as I know, there was no mention in the station records of any attack, a thousand years before I reported in, or any other time. And I think I'd know. I made it my business to familiarize myself with the station history as soon as I was assigned there."

"You didn't happen to notice any entry relating to the loss of a field man named Ravel?"

"If I did, it didn't register. The name meant nothing to me . . . then." Her eyes didn't quite meet mine.

"So we're talking about a class-one deviation. Either your past is aborted, or mine. The question is—which alternative is a part of the true timestem?"

"Insufficient data."

"Let's go on the next item: Nel Jard used an emergency system unknown to me to lift the entire station out of entropic context and deposit it in

what can be described as an achronic vacuole.
What that means I don't quite know."

"You're assuming it was Jard's action," Mellia
put in. "There's a possibility it wasn't. That another force stepped in just at that time, either to
complicate or annul his action. Did he say anything to indicate this was what he intended?" A tilt
of her head indicated the silent room where we
sat, and the ghostly void outside.

"He said something about null-time, but it didn't
really register. I thought he had old-fashioned demolition in mind; simple denial-to-the-enemy stuff."

"In any event, the station was shifted . . . here."

I nodded. "And when I used my emergency
jump gear, I homed in on it. I suppose that was to
be expected. I was tuned to the station frequency;
the equipment was designed for retrieval from any
space-time locus."

"You found the station empty—just as it is
now. . . ."

"Uh-huh. I wonder . . ." I looked around the
room. "Was my last visit before this one—or
after?"

"At least it wasn't simultaneous. You didn't meet
yourself."

"It ought to be possible to tell," I said. "The
local entropic flow seems to be normal; local time
is passing." I got up and wandered around the
room, looking for some evidence of my having
been there before. If there was any, I couldn't see
it. I turned back to the table—and there it was.

"The trays," I said. "They were here—on the
table."

Mellia looked at them, then at me. She looked a
little scared. Anachronisms affect you that way.

"The same two seats," I said. "The leftovers

didn't look too fresh—but they hadn't had time to decay."

"So—you're due here at any time."

"We have a few hours anyway. The stuff was dry on the trays." I gave her a we're-in-this-together look. "We could wait," I said, "and meet me."

"No!" Very sharp. "No" again, less urgently, but still definite. "We mustn't introduce any further paranomalies, you know that."

"If we stopped me from going back and interfering with my previous assignment——"

"You're talking nonsense, Ravel. Now who's forgotten what the Timesweep effort is all about? Putting patches on the patches is no good. You went back—you returned safely. Here you are. It would be stupid to risk that, on . . . on . . ."

"On the chance of saving the operation?"

Her eyes met mine. "We can't complicate matters further. You went back, let's leave it at that. The question is—what's our indicated course of action now?"

I sat down. "Where were we?"

"You found the station empty, with evidence of our—present—visit."

"So I did the only thing that occurred to me. I used the station facilities for a jump I hoped would put me back at Nexx Central. It didn't work. In the absence of a programmed target, I reverted back along my own timeline and ended ten years in my subjective past. A class-A paranomaly, breaking every regulation in the book."

"Regulations don't cover our situation," she said. "You had no control over matters. You did what seemed best."

"And blew a job that was successfully completed and encoded on the master timeplot ten years ago.

One curious item in that connection is that the Karg I was supposed to take out—and didn't—was the same one I hit in Buffalo. Which implies that the Buffalo sequence followed from the second version rather than the original one."

"Or what you're considering the alternate version. Maybe it isn't. Perhaps your doubling-back was assimilated as a viable element in the revised plot."

"In that case, you're right about not waiting here to intercept me. But if you're wrong . . ."

"We have to take a stand somewhere—somewhen. You jumped back to the beach after that, and we met. Query: Why did both you and I home in on the same temporal locus?"

"No comment."

"We're snarling hell out of the timelines, Ravel."

"Can't be helped. Unless you think we ought to Kamikaze."

"Don't be foolish. We have to do what we can. Which means examine the facts and plan a logical next step."

"Logical: that's a good one, Agent Gayl. When did logic ever have anything to do with Timesweep Ops?"

"We've made some progress," she said levelly, not rising to the bait, refusing the opportunity for a nice soul-scouring argument. "We know we have to be on our way, and without much delay."

"All right, I'll grant the point. Which leaves us a choice of two courses. We can use the station transfer booth."

"And end up somewhere back in our own pasts, complicating matters still further."

"Could be. Or we can recharge our personal gear and jump out at random."

"With no conception of where that might put us." She shivered and covered it with a gesture; a graceful lift of her chin that reminded me of another time, another place, another girl.

No, damn it—not another girl!

"Or," she said, "we could go together . . . as we did before."

"That wouldn't change anything, Mellia. We'd still be launching ourselves into the timestream with no target. We might find ourselves spinning end over end in a fog like the one outside—or worse."

"At least—" she started to say, and caught herself. *At least we'd be together*—I could almost hear the words.

"At least we won't be sitting here idle while the universe falls to pieces around us," she said instead.

"So—how do you vote?"

There was a long silence. She didn't look at me; then she did. She started to speak, hesitated.

"The booth," she said.

"Together, or one at a time?"

"Can the field handle both of us simultaneously?"

"I think so."

"Together. Unless you know a reason for separating."

"None at all, Mellia."

"Then it's settled."

"Right. Now finish your meal. It may be a while before we have another chance to eat."

My last item of preparation was a small crater gun from the armory. I strapped it to my wrist, just out of sight under the cuff. We went along the time-shielded transit tunnel to the transfer booth. All readings were normal; the circuits were ready to operate. Under normal conditions a passenger would be rotated painlessly and instantaneously out of the timestream into the extratemporal medium, and rerotated into normal space-time at the main reception room at Nexx Central. What would happen this time was an open question. Maybe we'd drop back down my timeline, and there'd be two of us aboard the sinking galleass; or maybe Mellia Gayl's gestalt would be stronger and we'd arrive at a point in her past where we hadn't arrived before, thus adding to the disaster that had hit us. Or possibly somewhere in between. Or nowhere at all . . .

"Next stop Nexx Central," I said, and ushered Mellia inside. I squeezed in after her.

"Ready?"

She nodded.

I pressed the *Transmit* button.

The explosion blew both of us into our component atoms.

◊ **21** ◊

"Or maybe not," I heard a voice croak. I recognized the voice; it was mine, somewhat the worse for wear but still on the job. "Some dream," I went on, giving myself the word. "Some hangover. Some headache."

"Trans-temporal shock is the technical term, I believe," Lisa said beside me.

My eyes snapped open; well, snap isn't quite the word. They unglued themselves and winced at the light and made out a face nearby. A nice face, heart-shaped, with big dark eyes and the prettiest smile in the world.

But not Lisa.

"Are you all right?" Mellia said.

"It's nothing that a month in the intensive care unit wouldn't clear up," I said and got an elbow under me and looked around. We were in a spacious room, long and high, like a banqueting hall, with a smooth gray floor, pale gray walls covered with row on row of instrument faces. Center position went to a big chair facing an array of display screens and a coding console. At the far end the open sky was visible through a glass wall.

"Where are we?"

"I don't know. Some sort of technical facility. You don't recognize it?"

I shook my head; if it was anything out of my past, the memory had been wiped clean.

"How long have I been out?" I asked.

"I woke up an hour ago."

I shook my head to clear it, and succeeded in sending pains like hot knives through my temples.

"Rough passage," I mumbled, and got to my feet. I felt sick and dizzy, as if I'd eaten too much ice cream on the merry-go-round.

"I've looked at some of the equipment," Mellia said. "Temporal gear, but not exactly like anything I've seen." Her tone suggested that meant something important. I tried to focus my brain and figure out what.

I said, "Oh."

"I could deduce the function of some of it," she said. "Some was completely baffling."

"Maybe it's Third Era stuff——"

"I'd recognize that."

"Let's take a look." I headed toward the big controller's chair, trying to look healthier than I felt. If the jump had affected Mellia at all, she didn't show it.

The console was covered with buttons labeled laconically with designations such as $M. Ds—H$ and $LV 3–gn$. The screens were the usual milky-glass anti-glare surfaces, set inside and anti-reflecting frames.

"They're ordinary analog-potential readout boards, of course," Mellia said, "but with two extra banks of controls—and that implies at least an additional order of sensitivity in the discretion and weighing circuitry."

"Does it?"

"Certainly." Her slim finger reached past me, tapped out a swift code on the colored keys. The screen twinkled and snapped to brightness.

"The pickup field is on active phase—or should be," she said. "But there's no base reading. And I'm afraid to play with a Timecast keybank I don't understand."

"You've left me in the shade," I said. "I never saw anything like this stuff. What else is there?"

"There are rooms back there." She pointed to the end of the hall opposite the glass wall. "Equipment rooms; a power section, operations . . ."

"Sounds like a regulation Timecasting station."

She nodded. "Almost."

"A little on the large side," I commented. "Let's take a look."

We went through rooms packed with gear as mysterious to me as a wiring diagram to I-Em Hotep. One contained nothing but three full-length mirrors; our reflections looking back at us were a couple of forlorn strangers. Nowhere were there any indications of recent habitation. No people, no signs of people. Just a dead building full of echoes.

We recrossed the grand hall and found an exit vestibule that cycled us out onto a wide stone terrace above a familiar view of sand and sea. The curve of the shoreline was as I had seen it last; only the jungle growth on the headland seemed denser, more solid somehow.

"Good old Dinosaur Beach," I said. "Doesn't change much, does it?"

"Time has passed," Mellia said. "A great deal of time."

"There was nothing like this in any projection plan I ever saw," I said. "Any ideas?"

"Not that I want to verbalize."

"I know how you feel," I said, and held the door for her. "By the way: I ought to tell you: I never heard of analog-potential. What is it, a new kind of breakfast food?"

"A-P is the basis of the entire Timesweep program," she said and looked at me sharply. "Any Nexx agent would have to be familiar with it." She was frowning at me pretty severely.

"Don't count on it," I said. "The lectures I got at the Institute were all about deterministics, actualization dynamics, and fixation levels."

"That's nonsense. Discredited Fatalistics Theory."

"Hold on, Miss Gayl, before you pop a valve. Don't look at me as if you'd caught me in the computer room with a live bomb. I admit I'm a little slow this morning, what with the heavy swell under the stern quarter, but I'm still the same sweet, lovable guy you fished out of the pond. I'm as much a Nexxman as you are; but a kind of dirty suspicion is sneaking up on me."

"And what might that be?"

"That the Nexx Central you work out of and the one I know aren't the same."

"That's ridiculous. The entire Nexx operation is based on the stability of the unique Nexx Baseline——"

"Sure—that's the concept. It won't be the first concept that had to be modified in the face of experience."

She looked a little pale. "You realize what you're implying?"

"Uh-huh. We've messed things up good, kid. For you and me to be standing here face to face—

representatives of two mutually exclusive base timetracks—means things are worse than we thought; worse than I knew they could be."

Her eyes held on mine, wide and shocked. I was doing a good job of reassuring her.

"But we're not licked yet," I said heartily. "We're still trained agents, still operational. We'll do the best we can——"

"That's not the point."

"Oh? What is?"

"We have a job to do—as you said: to attempt to reintroduce ourselves into the temporal pattern by eliminating the chronomalies we've unwittingly generated."

"Agreed."

"Very well—what pattern do we work toward, Ravel? Yours—or mine? It is a Deterministic or an A-P continuum we're supposed to be reassembling?"

I started to give her a fast, reassuring answer, but it stuck in my throat.

"We can work that out later," I said.

"How can we? Every move we make from this point on has to be correctly calculated. There's equipment here—" she waved a hand—"that's more sophisticated than anything I've ever seen. But we have to use it properly."

"Sure we do—but first we have to figure out what all the pretty little buttons are for. Let's concentrate on that for the present, Mellia. Maybe along the way we can resolve the philosophical questions."

"Before we can work together, we have to come to some agreement."

"Go on."

"I want your word you won't . . . do anything prejudicial to the A-P concept."

"I won't do anything without conferring with you first. As to what Universe it is we're rebuilding—let's wait until we know a little more before we commit ourselves, all right?"

She looked at me a long time before she said, "Very well."

"You might start," I said, "by explaining this setup to me."

She spent the next hour giving me a fast, sketchy, but graphic briefing on the art of analog-potential interpretation; I listened as fast as I could. The A-P theory was news to me, but I was accustomed to working with complex chronic gear. I began to get some idea of what the equipment was for.

"I get the feeling that your version of Nexx Central operates a lot farther out in the theoretical boondocks than the one I know," I said. "And backs it up with some very highly evolved hardware."

"Of course, what I'm accustomed to is much less advanced than this," Mellia said. "I don't know what to make of a lot of this."

"But you're sure it's A-P type gear?"

"There's no doubt in my mind at all. It couldn't be anything else—certainly not anything that Deterministic theory might have given rise to."

"I agree with that last point. This layout would make about as much sense at Central—my Central—as a steam whistle on a sailboat."

"Then you agree we have to work toward an A-P matrix?"

"Slow down, girl. You talk as if all we had to do was shake hands on it, and everything would switch back to where it was last Wednesday at three o'clock. We're working in the blind. We don't know what's happened, where we are, where we're going, or how to get there. Let's take it one item at a time. A good place to start would be this whole A-P concept. I get a strange feeling that its theoretical basis is a second-generation type of thing; that it arises from the kind of observational foundation generated by a major temporal realignment."

"Would you mind clarifying that?" she said coldly.

I waved a hand. "Your Central isn't on the main timestem. It's too complex, too artificial. It's like a star with a large heavy-element content: it can't arise from the primordial dust cloud. It has to be formed out of stellar debris from a previous generation."

"That's a rather fanciful analogy. Is that the best you can do?"

"On such short notice. Or would you rather have me suppress anything that seems to cast doubts on your A-P universe as the best of all possible worlds?"

"That's unfair."

"Is it? I've got a stake in my past, too, Miss Gayl. I'm not any more eager to be relegated to the realms of unrealized possibilities than anybody else."

"I . . . I didn't mean that. What makes you think—there's no reason to believe——"

"I have a funny feeling there's no place for me in your world-picture, Mellia. Your original world-picture, that is. I'm the guy who loused up the sweet serenity of Dinosaur Beach. But for me, the old outfit would have been in operation for another thousand years at the same address."

She started to say something, but I steam-rollered it.

"But it wasn't. I fouled up my assignment—don't ask me how—and as a result, blew the station to Kingdom Come—or wherever it disappeared to——"

"You don't need to blame yourself. You carried out your instructions; it wasn't your fault if the results . . . if after you came back . . ."

"Yeah. If what I did started a causal chain that resulted in your not being born. But you *were* born, L—Mellia. I met you on a cover assignment in 1936. So at that point, at least, we were on the same track. Or—" I cut it off there, but she saw the same thing I did.

"Or perhaps . . . your whole sequence in Buffalo was an aborted loop. Not part of the Main Tape. Not viable."

"It's viable, baby. You can depend on it." I ground that out like a rock crusher reducing boulders to number nine gravel.

"Of course," she whispered. "It's Lisa, isn't it? She *has* to be real. Any alternative is unthinkable. And if that means remaking the space-time continuum, aborting a thousand years of Timestem history, wrecking Timesweep and all it means—why, that's a small price to pay for the existence of your beloved!"

"You said it. I didn't."

She looked at me the way a tough engineer looks at a hill that's standing where he wants to build a level crossing.

"Let's get to work," she said at last in a voice from which every shred of emotion had been scraped.

◇ **22** ◇

We spent the rest of the day making a methodical survey of the installation. It was four times the size of the Dinosaur Beach stations we had known in our previous incarnations; and 80 percent of it was given over to gear that neither of us understood. Mellia pieced together the general plan of the station, identified the major components of the system, traced out the power transfer apparatus, deduced the meanings of some of the cryptic legends at the control consoles. I followed her and listened.

"It doesn't make much sense," she said. It was twilight, and a big red sun was casting long shadows across the floor. "The power supply is out of all proportion to any intelligence-input or interpretative function I can conceive. And all this space—what's it for, Ravel? What is this place?"

"Grand Central Station," I said.

"What's that?"

"Nothing. Just a forgotten building in a forgotten town that probably never existed. A terminal."

"You may be right," she said, sounding thoughtful. "If this were all designed to transfer bulk cargo, rather than merely as a communications and personnel staging facility . . ."

"Cargo. What kind of cargo?"

"I don't know. It doesn't sound likely, does it? Any appreciable inter-local material transfer would tend to weaken the temporal structure at both transmission and reception points. . . ."

"Maybe they didn't care anymore. Maybe they were like me: tired." I yawned. "Let's turn in; maybe tomorrow it will all turn into sweet reasonableness before our startled gaze."

"What did you mean by that remark? About not caring?"

"Who me? Not a thing, girl, not a thing."

"Did you ever call Lisa 'girl'?" This sharply.

"What's that got to do with anything?"

"It has everythng to do with everything! Everything you say and do—everything you think—is colored by your idiotic infatuation with this . . . this figmentary sweetheart! Can't you forget her and put your mind on the fact that the Nexx Timestem is in desperate danger—if it's not irreparably damaged—by your irresponsible actions!"

"No," I said between my teeth. "Any other questions?"

"I'm sorry," she said in a spent voice. She put a hand over her face and shook her head. "I didn't mean that. I'm just tired . . . so very tired—and frightened."

"Sure," I said. "Me too. Forget it. Let's get some sleep."

We picked separate rooms. Nobody bothered to say good night.

◊ **23** ◊

I got up early; even asleep, the silence got to me. There was a well-equipped kitchen at the end of the dormitory wing; apparently even A-P theoreticians had a taste for a fresh-laid egg and a slice of sugar-cured ham from a nulltime locker where aging didn't happen.

I punched in two breakfasts and started back to call Mellia, and then changed my mind when I heard footsteps across the big hall.

She was standing by the Timecaster's chair, dressed in a loose robe, looking at the screen. She didn't hear me coming, barefooted, until I was within ten feet of her. She turned suddenly, and from the expression on her face, nearly had an angina attack.

So did I. It wasn't Mellia's beautiful if disapproving face; it was an old woman, white-haired, with sunken cheeks and faded eyes that might have been bright and passionate once, a long time ago. She tottered, as if she were going to fall, and I shot out a hand and caught her by an arm as thin as a stick of wood inside her flowing sleeve. She made a nice recovery; feature by feature, her face put itself back together, leaving a look that was almost too serene, under the circumstances.

"Yes," she said, in a thin, old, but very calm voice. "You've come. As I knew you would, of course."

"It's nice to be expected, ma'am," I said inanely. "Who told you? About us, I mean. Coming, that is."

A flicker of a frown went across her face. "The predictor screens, of course." Her eyes went past me. "May I ask: where is the rest of your party?"

"She's, ah, still asleep."

"Asleep? How very curious."

"Back there." I nodded toward the bedrooms. "She'll be happy to know we aren't alone here. We had a long day yesterday, and——"

"Excuse me. Yesterday? When did you come?"

"About twenty-four hours ago."

"But—why didn't you advise me at once? I've been waiting—I've been ready . . . for such a long time . . ." Her voice almost broke, but she caught it.

"I'm sorry, ma'am. We didn't know you were here. We searched the place, but——"

"You didn't *know*?" Her face looked shocked, stricken.

"Where were you keeping yourself? I thought we'd checked every room. . . ."

"I . . . my . . . I have my quarters in the outwing," she said in a broken voice. A tear spilled from the outer corner of each eye and she brushed them away impatiently. "I had assumed," she said, getting her voice under control again, "that you had come in response to my signal. But of course that's not important. You're here. May I have just a few minutes? There are some things—mementos—but if there's any hurry, I can leave them, of course," she added hurriedly, watching my face.

"I have no intention of hurrying you, ma'am," I said. "But I think there may be some misunderstanding——"

"But you *will* take me?" Her thin hand caught my arm; panic was in her voice. "Oh, please, take me with you, I beg you, please, don't leave me here——"

"I promise," I said, and put my hand over hers; it was as cool and thin as a turkey's foot.

"But I think you're making some erroneous assumptions. Maybe I did too. Are you a part of the station cadre?"

"Oh, no." She shook her head like a child caught with a paw in the cookie jar. "This is not my station. Not my station at all. I merely took refuge here, you see, after the collapse."

"Where are the station personnel, ma'am?"

She looked at me as if I'd said something amazing. "There are none. No one. It's as I stated in my reports. I found the station abandoned. I've been here alone, no one else——"

"Sure, I see, just you. Pretty lonely. But it's all right now, we're here, you won't be alone any longer."

"Yes, you're here. As I knew you would be—someday. The instruments never lie. That's what I told myself. It was just that I didn't know *when*."

"Instruments—told you we'd come?"

"Oh, yes."

She sank into the nearest chair, and her old fingers flew over the keys. The screen lit up, changed texture, flowed through colors, ended a vivid greenish-white rectangle on the right edge of which a wavering black vertical line, like a scratch on a film strip, flickered and danced. I was about to open my mouth to admire her virtuosity on the keyboard when she made a small sighing sound and crumpled forward onto her face, out cold.

I grabbed her, eased her from the chair, got my arms under her. She couldn't have weighed ninety pounds. Mellia met me at the mouth of the corridor. She stopped dead and put a hand over her mouth, then remembered her Field Agent's training and smoothed the look off her face.

"Ravel—who——"

"Dunno. She was here when I woke up; thought I'd come to rescue her. She started to tell me something, and fainted."

Mellia stepped back to let me pass, her eyes on the old woman. She stiffened; she caught my arm. She stared at the withered face.

"Mother!" she gasped.

◇ **24** ◇

I let a few long seconds slide past. The old lady's eyes fluttered and opened. "Mother!" Mellia said again and grabbed for her hand.

The old lady smiled rather vaguely. "No, no, I'm not anyone's mother," she said. "I always wanted . . . but . . ." She faded out again.

I took her along to an empty room and put her on the bed. Mellia sat beside her and rubbed her hands and made sure she was breathing properly.

"What's this about your mother?" I said.

"I'm sorry. She's not my mother, of course. I was just being silly. I suppose all elderly women look alike . . ."

"Is your mother that old?"

"No, of course not. It was just a superficial resemblance." She gave me a small apologetic laugh. "I suppose the psychologists could read all sorts of things into it."

"She said she was expecting us," I said. "Said the instruments predicted it."

Mellia looked at me. "Predicted? There's no such instrument."

"Maybe she's slipped her clutch. Alone too long."

The old lady sighed and opened her eyes again. If Lisa reminded her of anyone, she didn't say so. Mellia made encouraging noises. They smiled at each other. Love at first sight.

"Now I've made an old fool of myself," the old lady said. "Fainting like that . . ." Her expression became troubled.

"Don't be silly," Mellia said. "It's perfectly understandable. . . ."

"Do you feel well enough to talk?" I said, in spite of the dirty look Mellia gave me.

"Of course."

I sat on the side of the bed. "Where are we?" I asked as gently as possible. "What is this place?"

"The Dinosaur Beach Timecast station," the old girl said, looking just a little surprised.

"Maybe I should say *when* are we . . ."

"The station date is twelve thirty-two." Now she looked puzzled.

"But—" Mellia said.

"Meaning we haven't made a Timejump after all," I told her, as smoothly as you can say something as preposterous as that.

"Then—we've jumped—somehow—to a secondary line!"

"Not necessarily. Who's to say what's primary and what's secondary, after what we've been through?"

"Excuse me," the old lady said. "I get the impression from what you say that . . . that matters are not as well as might be hoped."

Mellia gave me a troubled look. I passed it on to the old lady.

"It's quite all right," she said. "You may speak freely to me . . . I understand that you are Timecast

agents. That makes us colleagues." She smiled
faintly.

"Field Agent Mellia Gayl, at your service," she
said.

◊ **25** ◊

I happened to be looking at Mellia—*my* Mellia; her face turned as pale as marble. She didn't move, didn't speak.

"And who are you, my dear?" the old lady said, almost gaily. She couldn't see Mellia's face. "I almost feel I know you."

"I'm Field Agent Ravel," I spoke up. "This is— Agent Lisa Kelly."

Mellia turned on me, but caught herself. I watched her smoothing her face out; it was an admirable piece of work.

"We're happy to meet . . . a . . . a colleague, Agent Gayl," she said in a voice with all the color washed out of it.

"Oh, yes, I led a very active life at one time," the old lady said, lightly, smiling. "Life was exciting in those days, before . . . before the Collapse. We had such high ambitions, such a noble program. How we worked and planned! After each mission, we'd gather to study the big screen, to gauge the effects of our efforts, to congratulate or commiserate with each other. We had such *hopes* in those days."

"I'm sure you did," Mellia said in a lifeless whisper.

"After the official announcement, of course, things were different," the elderly Miss Gayl went on. "We still tried, of course; we hadn't really accepted defeat, admitted it; but we knew. And then . . . the deterioration began. The chronodegradation. Little things, at first. The loss of familiar articles, the memory lapses, and the contradictions. We sensed life unraveling around us. Many of the personnel began dropping off, then. Some jumped out to what they hoped might be stable loci; others were lost in temporal distortion areas. Some simply—deserted, wandered away. I stayed on, of course. I always hoped—somehow—" She broke off abruptly. "But all that's neither here nor there, of course——"

"No—please. Go on," young Mellia said.

"Why—there's little more to tell. The time came when there were only a handful of us left at Central. We agreed it was impossible to attempt to keep the transmitters in operation any longer. We'd made no personnel retrieval for over a year, the equipment was chronodegrading at an accelerating rate, there was no way of knowing what additional damage we might be doing to the temporal fabric with our improperly tuned gear. So—we shut down. After that, matters swiftly deteriorated. Abnormal manifestations increased. Conditions became—difficult. We out-jumped, and found matters in an even worse state elsewhere—and elsewhen. I'm afraid we panicked. I know I did. I admit it now— though at the time I told myself I was searching for a configuration where I might attempt to rally

stablizing forces—but that was mere rationalization. I jumped out—and out. At last—I arrived
here. To me it seemed a haven of peace and
stability. Empty, of course—but safe. For a while
I was almost happy—until, of course, I discovered
I was trapped." She looked up at me and smiled a
frail smile.

"Twice I tried to escape," she whispered. "Each
time—after horrifying experiences—I ended back
here. Then I knew. I had entered a closed loop. I
was caught—until someone came to set me free.
So—I . . . settled down to wait." She gave me a
look that made me feel as if I'd just kicked a
cripple down the stairs.

"You seem to be familiar with the equipment," I
said, just to fill the conversational gap.

"Oh, yes, I've had ample time to explore its
capabilities. Its potential capabilities, that is to
say. Under the circumstances, of course, only minimal environmental monitor functions are possible—
such as the forecast vectors that indicated that one
day help would come." The smile again, as if I was
Lindy and I'd just flown an ocean, all for her.

"The screen you activated," I said, "I've never
seen one just like it. Is it the one that, ah, foretells
the future?"

"Screen?" she looked puzzled. Then recollec-
tion came; she gasped and sat up suddenly. "I
must check——"

"No, no, you need to rest!" Mellia protested.

"Help me up, my dear. I *must* confirm the
read-out!"

Mellia started to argue, but I caught her eye
and together we helped our patient to her feet,
along the corridor.

The lighted screen was still the same: a rectan-

gle of green luminosity with a ragged edge that
rippled and danced on the extreme right. The old
lady gave a weak cry and clutched our hands.

"What is it?" Mellia asked.

"The Maintrunk forecast carrier!" she quavered.
"It's gone—off the screen!"

"Maybe an adjustment—" I started.

"No! The reading is true," she said in a voice
that suddenly had a faint echo of what had once
been a snap of authority. "A terminal reading!"

"What does it mean?" Mellia asked in a soothing
tone. "Surely it can't be that serious——"

"It means we've come to the end of the temporal segment we're occupying. That for us—time is
coming to an end."

"You're sure of this?" I asked.

"Quite sure."

"How long?"

"It may be hours, or minutes," the old Mellia
said. "I think this is a contingency the makers of
the equipment never anticipated occurring." She
gave me a calm, self-contained look. "If you have
transfer capability to any secondary trunk, I suggest you use it without delay."

I shook my head. "No, we shot our final bolt
getting here. We're stranded."

"Of course. At infinity all lines converge at a
point. Time ends; so must all else."

"What about the station transfer facilities?" Mellia
asked. Agent Gayl shook her head.

"I tried; it's fruitless. You'd endure needless
horrors—for nothing."

"Still——"

"She's right," I said. "There'll be nothing for us
there. We need another approach. All this equipment—isn't there something here that can be

used—converted, maybe—to crack us out of this
dead end?"

"Perhaps—if one were technically trained," the
old Mellia said vaguely. "But it's far beyond my
competence."

"We can recharge our personal fields," I said,
and felt a sudden change in the atmosphere. So
did Mellia—both of her. The screen *flick-flick-
flicked* and died. The indicator lights faded, all
across the panels. The background sounds dwindled into silence. The color of the air changed,
became a dirty electric translucence. Tiny waves
of color seemed to ripple across the surfaces of
objects, like chromatic aberration in a cheap lens.
A chill struck through the air as if someone had
just opened a giant refrigerator door.

"It's the end," the elderly Mellia said, quite
calmly now. "Time ceases, all wave phenomena
drop to a zero frequency, and thus become nonexistent—including that special form of energy we
call matter. . . ."

"Just a minute," I said. "This is no natural
phenomenon. Someone's manipulating the chro-
nocosm!"

"How do you know that?" Mellia asked.

"No time for conversation. Agent Gayl"—I took
the old lady's arm—"where were you when we
arrived?"

Mellia started to protest, but the other Mellia
answered promptly: "In the stasis vault."

"The mirrors?"

She nodded. "I was . . . ashamed to tell you. It
seemed so . . . cowardly."

"Come on." I led the way across the big room,
through the silence and the cold and the dead air,

down the passage to the hall of mirrors. The reflective surfaces were tarnished, but still intact.

"Quickly!" the old Mellia said. "The fields will break down at any moment!"

Sounds came from the direction of the big room: a crash as of falling masonry, curiously muffled; a heavy rumbling. A slow cloud of smoke or dust bulged leisurely along the passage. Yellow light glowed behind it.

"Inside—fast!" I said to Mellia.

"No—you and . . . Agent Gayl!"

"Don't argue, girl!" I caught her in my arms, pushed her toward the mirror. Waves of dull color ran across it. Mellia struggled.

"Mr. Ravel—you must go—now!" the elder Mellia said, and turned quickly and walked back toward the advancing dust-roil. Mellia cried out; I thrust her through the mirror. Her cry cut off sharply.

The old lady was gone, invisible beyond the obscuring cloud. I stepped to the other mirror; it felt like cold fog. It shimmered around me, cloying like impalpable gray gelatin, flashed like exploding glass. Darkness closed in.

For a moment I was aware of a sense of breathless expectancy, like the instant after the disaster becomes apparent and before the first shock arrives.

Then nothing.

◊ **26** ◊

A yellow light was shining through the murk. I didn't know how long it had been shining. It grew brighter, and a man appeared silhouetted against it, walking slowly forward, as if against resistance.

When he was six feet away, I saw my mistake.

Not a man. A Karg. The same one I'd killed twice and let get away a third time.

I couldn't move a muscle, not even my eyes. I watched the Karg cross my field of vision. I wasn't breathing; if my heart was beating, I couldn't feel it. But I was conscious. That was something.

The Karg was moving with effort, but unconcernedly. He was dressed in a plain black skin suit with harness and attachments. He looked at an array of miniature meters strapped to his wrist—the underside—and made an adjustment. So far he had paid no more attention to me than as if I were a piece of bric-a-brac.

Now he came over to me and looked me over. His baby-blue eyes never quite met mine—not from embarrassment, just indifference. Two other men—not Kargs—came into view. They ploughed

116

their way up to him, conferred. The newcomers were carrying something that looked like bundled shingles. They came on across to me, moved around behind me, all this in total silence. Some time passed—or maybe it didn't. From the corner of my eye I saw movement. A panel slid into position to my left. It was dark green, glassy. Another appeared on my right. One of the men entered my field of vision, carrying a three-by-six sheet of thin material. He stood it on end; it stood by itself in mid-air without support. He pushed it in front of me and closed off my view. Light showed at its edges; then it snapped into place and left me in a darkness like the inside of a paint can.

With the visual reference gone, I lost my sense of orientation. I was upside down, spinning slowly—or not so slowly; I was a mile high, I was an inch high, I filled the universe, I didn't exist——

With a crash, sound returned to the world, along with gravity, pains all over like a form-fitting suit studded with needles, and suffocation. I dragged hard and got a breath in, feeling my heart start to thump and wheeze in its accustomed way. The roar faded without fading; it was just the impact of air molecules whanging against my eardrums, I realized: a background sound that was ordinarily filtered out automatically.

My knee bumped the wall in front of me. I was bracing myself to give it a kick when it fell away and I stepped out into a big room with high purple-black walls, where three people waited for me with expressions that were more intent than welcoming.

One was a short, thick-fingered man in a gray smock, with thin hair, ruddy features, rubbery lips stretched back over large off-white teeth. Number two was a woman, fortyish, a little on the lean side, very starched and official in dark green. The third was the Karg, dressed now in a plain gray coverall.

Shorty stepped forward and thrust out a hand; he held it in a curiously awkward position, with the fingers spread and pointed down. I shook it once and he took it back and examined it carefully, as if he thought I might have left a mark.

"Welcome to Dinosaur Beach Station," the Karg said in a reasonable facsimile of a friendly voice. I looked around the room; we were the only occupants.

"Where are the two women?" I asked. The thick man looked blank and pulled at his rubbery lip. The female looked back at me as if it was all academic to her.

"Perhaps Dr. Javeh will wish to explain matters." She sounded as if she doubted it.

"I'm not interested in having a conversation with a machine," I said. "Who programs it? You?" I aimed this last at Rubber-lips.

"Whaaat?" he said, and looked at the woman; she looked at the Karg; it looked at me. I looked at all of them.

"Dr. Javeh is our Chief of Recoveries," the woman said quickly, as if glossing over a small social blunder on my part. "I'm Dr. Fresca; and this is Administrator Koska."

"There were two women with me, Dr. Fresca," I said. "Where are they?"

"I'm sure I have no idea; this is hardly my area of competence."

"Where are they, Koska?"

His lips worked, snapping from a smile to dismay and back. "As to that, I can only refer you to Dr. Javeh——"

"You take orders from this Karg?"

"I'm not familiar with that term." Stiffly; the smile gone.

I faced the Karg. He looked blandly at me with his pale blue eyes.

"You're a bit disoriented," he said quietly. "Not surprising, of course, they often are——"

"Who's 'they'?"

"The recoverees. That's my work—our work, you understand: detecting, pinpointing, and retrieving personnel in, ah, certain circumstances."

"Who's your boss, Karg?"

He cocked his head. "I'm sorry; I don't understand your repeated use of the term 'Karg.' Just what does it signify?"

"It signifies that whatever these people believe, I'm on to you."

He smiled and lifted his hands, let them fall back. "As you will. As for my supervisor—I happen to be Officer-in-Charge here."

"Cosy," I said. "Where are the two women?"

The Karg's little rosebud mouth tightened. "I have no idea to whom you refer."

"They were with me—five minutes ago. You must have seen them."

"I'm afraid you don't quite understand the situation," the Karg said. "When I found you, you were quite alone. The indications suggest you had been adrift in the achronic void for an extended period."

"How long?"

"Ah, a most interesting problem in temporal relativistics. We have biological time, unique to the individual, metered in heartbeats; and psychological time, a purely subjective phenomenon in which seconds can seem like years, and the reverse. But as to your question: The Final Authority has established a calibration system for gauging absolute duration; and in terms of that system, your sojourn outside the entropic stream endured for a period in excess of a century, with an observational error of plus or minus 10 percent, I should say."

The Karg spread his uncalloused hands, smiled a philosophical smile.

"As for your, ah, female—I know nothing."

I swung on him; the swing didn't connect, but I got the crater gun into my hand unseen. The Karg ducked back and Dr. Fresca let out a yelp and Koska grabbed my arm. The Karg flicked something at me that smacked my side wetly and spread and grabbed my arms and suddenly I was wrapped to the knees in what looked like spider webs, white as spun candy, smelling of a volatile polyester.

I tried to take a step and almost fell, and Koska stepped forward to assist me to a chair, all very solicitously, as if I'd had one of my fainting spells, but I'd be all right in a minute.

"You're a liar, Karg," I said, "and a bad one. It takes a live man to perjure himself with that true ring of sincerity. You didn't grapple me out of a few billion square millennia of eternity at random. They did a nice job on your scars, but you know me. And if you know me, you know her."

The Karg looked thoughtful; he motioned, and Koska and the woman left the room without a backward glance. He faced me with a different expression on his plastalloy features.

"Very well, Mr. Ravel, I know you. Not personally; your reference to scars presumably applies to some confrontation which has been relegated to the status of the unrealized possibility. But I know you by reputation, by profession. As for the woman—possibly I can look into the matter of a search for her later—after we've reached an understanding." He was just a Karg now, all business and no regrets.

"I already understand you, Karg," I said.

"Let me tell you of our work, Mr. Ravel," he said mildly. "I think when you understand fully you'll want to contribute wholeheartedly to our great effort."

"Don't bet on it, Karg," I said.

"Your hostility is misplaced," the Karg said. "We here at Dinosaur Beach have need of your abilities and experience, Mr. Ravel——"

"I'll bet you do. Who are your friends? Third Era dropouts? Or are you recruiting all the way back to Second Era now?"

The Karg ignored that. "Through my efforts," he said, "you've been given an opportunity to carry on the work to which your life was devoted. Surely you see that it's in your interest to co-operate?"

"I doubt that your interests and mine could ever coincide, Karg."

"Conditions have changed, Mr. Ravel. It's necessary for all of us to realign our thinking in terms of the existent realities."

"Tell me about them."

"Your great Nexx Timesweep effort failed, of course, as I'm sure you've deduced by now. It was a noble undertaking, but misguided, as others before it. The true key to temporal stability lies not in a simple effort to restore the past to its virgin state, but in making intelligent use of the facilities and resources existent in that portion of the entropic spectrum available to us to create and maintain a viable enclave of adequate dimensions to support the full flowering of the racial destiny. To this end the final Authority was established, with the mission of salvaging from every era all that could be saved from the debacle of aborted temporal progression. I'm pleased to be able to tell you that our work has proved a great success."

"So you're looting up and down the temporal core, and setting up housekeeping—where?"

"The Final Authority has set aside a reservation of ten centuries in what was formerly known as Old Era time. As for your use of the the term 'looting'—you yourself, Mr. Ravel, are an example of the chief object of our Recovery Service."

"Men—and women. All trained agents, I suppose."

"Of course."

"And all of them are so happy to be here that they turn their talents to building this tight little island in time you seem so happy with."

"Not all, Mr. Ravel. But a significant number."

"I'll bet it's significant. Mostly ex-Third Era and prior Timesweep types, eh? Sophisticated enough to realize that matters are in a bad way, but not quite sophisticated enough to realize that what you're building around yourself is just a sterile dead end."

"I fail to understand your attitude, Mr. Ravel. Sterile? You are free to breed; plants grow, the sun shines, chemical reactions occur."

I laughed. "Spoken like a machine, Karg. You just don't get the point do you?"

"The point is to preserve rational life in the universe," he said patiently.

"Uh-huh—but not in a museum, under a glass case and a layer of fine dust. Perpetual motion is an exploded theory, Karg. Going round and round in a temporal loop—even a loop a thousand years long—isn't quite my idea of human destiny."

"Nevertheless, you will lend your support to the Final Authority."

"Will I?"

"You would, I believe, find the alternative most unpleasant."

"Pleasant, unpleasant. Just words, Karg." I looked around the big, gloomy room. It was cold, with a feeling of dampness, as if the walls ought to be beaded with condensation. "This is where you explain to me how you're going to go to work with the splinters under the fingernails, and the thumb-press, and the rack. And then go on to explain how you're going to make sure I behave, after you send me out on an assignment."

"No physical persuasions will be needed, Mr. Ravel. You will perform as required in order to earn the reward I offer. Agent Gayl was recovered some time ago. It was through her inquiries that I became interested in you. I assured her that in return for her efforts on behalf of the Final Authority, I would undertake to locate and recover you."

"I don't suppose you've gotten around to telling her you found me?"

"That would not be to the advantage of the Final Authority at this time."

"So you keep her on the string while you work both sides of the street."

"That's correct."

"One nice thing about working with a piece of machinery: you don't waste time trying to justify your actions."

"The personnel with whom I work are not aware

of the artificial nature of my origin, Mr. Ravel. As you surmise, they are largely Second Era. It is not in the best interest of the Authority that they be so apprised."

"What if I tell them anyway?"

"I will then bring Agent Gayl into your presence and there execute her."

"What—and waste all the effort you've put into this program?"

"Less than total control is no control at all. You will obey my instructions, Mr. Ravel. In every detail. Or I will scrap the project."

"Neat, logical, and to the point," I said. "You just missed one thing."

"What might that be?"

"This," I said, and lifted the crater gun and fired from the hip, the only place I could fire from with my arms bound to my sides. It wasn't a clean shot; but it blew his knee into rags and sent him across the room on his back.

By a combination of flopping and rolling, I got to him while his electroneuronic system was still in fibrillation, got his chest panel open and thumbed the switch that put him on manual.

"Lie quietly," I said, and he relaxed, looking at nothing.

"Where's the unlock for this tanglenet?"

He told me. I worked the ballpoint pen projector out of his breast pocket and squirted a fine pink mist at the nearest portion of the goo I was wrapped in. It turned to putty, then to caked dust that I brushed away.

I cut the seals and lifted out his tape. He'd been modified to take an oversized cartridge, an endless loop designed to repeat automatically, estimated duration a hundred years plus.

Somebody had gone to a lot of trouble to put a self-servicing, non-terminating robot on the job.

A scanner was included in the installed equipment. I inserted the cartridge and set it at high speed and listened to a routine parameter-conditioning program, slightly amended here and there to override what had always been the basics of human-Karg relationships. It was logical enough: this Karg had been designed to operate in the total absence of human supervision.

I edited out the command and initiative portions of the tape and reinserted it.

"Where's the woman?" I asked. "Agent Mellia Gayl."

"I do not know," he said.

"Tsk," I said. "And she was supposed to be the bait to keep me in line. Lying again, Karg. It's a nasty habit but I know the cure for it." I asked him a few more questions, got the expected answers. He and his staff of Kargs and salvaged early-era humans had marooned themselves on a tight little island in a rising sea of entropic dissolution. They'd be safe here for a while—until the rot now nibbling at the edges reached the last year, the last day, the last hour. Then they'd be gone and all their works with them into the featureless homogeneity of the Ylem.

"It's a sad little operation you're running here, Karg," I told it. "But don't worry: nothing lasts forever."

He didn't answer. I snooped around the room for a few minutes longer, recording what interested me; I could have made good use of that breakfast I hadn't eaten, a hundred years ago; and there were all sorts of special equipment that could be useful where I was going; and maybe there were a few more questions that should have been asked. But I had the feeling that the sooner I departed from the jurisdiction of the Final Authority the better it would be for me and whatever was left of my aspirations.

"Any last words for posterity?" I asked the Karg. "Before I effect that cure I mentioned?"

"You will fail," he said.

"Maybe," I said. "By the way, push your self-destruct button."

He obeyed; smoke started rising from his interior. I referred to the homing signaler I had tuned to Mellia Gayl, read out the correct co-ordinates. I unlocked the transfer booth and punched in my destination, stepped inside the booth and activated the sender field. Reality shattered into a million splinters and reassembled itself in another shape, another time, another place.

I was just in time.

◇ **27** ◇

It was a windy hillside, under a low gray sky. Green grass, black moss, bare rock, weathered smooth. A herd of dirty yellow-gray sheep in the middle distance against a backdrop of rounded hills. And in the foreground a crowd all set to lynch a witch.

There were about three dozen people, of the rude but hearty villager variety, dressed in motley costumes of coarse cloth that suggested a raid on a ragpicker's wagon. Most of them had sticks or wooden farm implements; a few had handcarved shillelaghs, well polished by use; and all of them had expressions of innocent ferocity. The expressions were aimed at Mellia, who occupied a central position with her hands tied behind her, wrapped halfway to the elbow in heavy brown rope.

She was dressed in gray homespun, and the wind flapped her long skirts, blew her red-brown hair around her shoulders like a flag of no surrender. A tossed stone hit her a glancing blow on the face, and she stumbled, caught herself, stared back

127

at them with her chin high and a bright trickle of
blood on her cheek. Then she caught sight of me.
If I was expecting a gladsome smile of welcome, I
was disappointed. She looked straight into my eyes;
then she turned her back.

A wide-shouldered man reached out a big square
hand and clamped it on her shoulder to spin her
around. I pushed a couple of committee members
aside and kicked him hard in the left calf. He
yelled and came around fast, hopping on one foot,
and gave me a nice shot at a bulgy red nose. It
splattered satisfactorily under a straight right, followed by a left hook that put him down on the
turf. Somebody started a yell, and I pivoted right
and got him square in the mouth with the edge of
my forearm. He backed off two steps and sat down
hard, spitting blood and maybe a tooth or two.

"You fool! You blind fool!" Mellia said, and over
my shoulder I snapped, "Shut up!"

They were recovering from their surprise now.
A few of the sharper ones began to suspect the
party was about over. They didn't like that. There
was a surge toward me, a tide of ugly, angry faces,
all chapped lips and bad teeth and broken veins
and glaring eyes. I'd had enough of them. I snapped
a *hold* on them, which I should have done in the
first place, and they froze hard in midyelp.

Mellia was caught in the *hold* field too, of course.
I picked her up carefully; it's easy to break bones
under those circumstances. Walking downhill was
like walking under water. On a packed-dirt road at
the bottom I put her on her feet and killed the
field. She staggered, gave me a wild look which
lacked any element of gratitude.

"How . . . did you do that?" she gasped.

"I have hidden talents. What were they on to

you for? Putting spells on cows?" I dabbed at the streak of blood on her face. She leaned away from my touch.

"I . . . violated their customs. They were merely carrying out the traditional punishment. It wouldn't have been fatal. And now you've ruined it all—destroyed everything I'd accomplished!"

"How do you like the idea you're working for a Karg named Dr. Javeh?"

She looked startled, then indignant.

"That's right," I said. "He fished you out of the void and sicked you onto this job."

"You're out of your mind! I broke out of stasis on my own; this is my program——"

"Un-unh, lady. He planted the idea on you. You've been working for a Karg—and a rogue Karg at that. He'd rewired himself and added a few talents his designers wouldn't have appreciated. Very cute. Or maybe somebody did it for him. It doesn't matter much——"

"You're talking nonsense!" She glared at me, looking for an opening to bring up what was really on her mind. "I suppose *she* didn't matter, either," she blurted, with charming feminine illogic.

"The elderly Agent Gayl? No, you're right. She didn't. She knew that——"

"You killed her! You saved yourself instead! You coward! You miserable coward!"

"Sure—anything you say, kid. But I only saved one of my skins; you seem to be dead set on keeping the whole collection intact."

"What——"

"You know what. When you get all choked up about the old lady it's yourself you're grieving for. She's you—fifty years on. You know it and I know it. Maybe she knew it too, and was too kind to let on. She was quite a girl, old Mellia was. And smart enough to know when it was time to take a fall."

"And you let her."

"I couldn't have stopped her—and I wouldn't have. Funny: you're jealous of yourself as Lisa, but you go all wivery over another aspect of your infinite versatility who spent a long and wasted life waiting for a chance to do something effective—and finally did it. I guess the shrinks could read something into that."

She nearly got her claws into my face; I held her off and nodded toward the crowd stringing down the hill.

"The audience want their money back," I said, "or another crack at the action. You say which. If you want to ride a rail buck naked in this wind, I'll say Excuse me, and be on my way."

"You're horrible! You're hard, cynical—merciless! I misjudged you; I thought——"

"Save the thoughts till later. Are you with them—or with me?"

She looked up the hill and shuddered.

"I'll go with you," she said in a dull, defeated voice.

I switched on my interference screen, which gave us effective invisibility.

"Stay close to me," I said. "Which way is the next town?"

She pointed. We set off at a brisk walk while the mob behind us yowled their wonder and their frustration.

◇ 28 ◇

It was a nasty little village, poverty-stricken, ugly, hostile, much like little towns in all times and climes.

"You forgot to mention where we are," I said.

"Wales; near Llandudno. 1723."

"You can sure pick'em, ma'am—if you like 'em dreary, that is."

I found a tavern under a sign with a crude pictorial representation of a pregnant woman in tears, and letters which spelled, more or less, Ye Weepinge Bride.

"Suits the mood exactly," I said, and switched off the I-field. A drizzling rain spattered us as we ducked under the low lintel. It was a dark little room, lit by a small coal fire on the hearth and a lantern hanging at one end of the plank bar. The floor was stone, damp, and uneven.

There were no other customers. A gnarly old man no more than four and a half feet tall watched us take chairs at a long oak table by one wall, under the lone window, all of a foot square and almost opaque with dirt, set just under the rafters. He

131

came shuffling across, looking us over with an expression in which any approval he may have felt was well concealed. He muttered something. I gave him a glare and barked, "What's that? Speak up, gaffer!"

"Y'be English, I doubt not," he growled.

"Then ye be a bigger fool than ye need be. Bring ale, stout ale, mind, and bread and meat. Hot meat—and fresh bread and white!"

He mumbled again. I scowled and reached for an imaginary dirk.

"More of ye'r insolence and I'll cut out ye'r heart and buy off the bailiff after," I snarled.

"Have you lost your mind?" Miss Gayl started to say, in the twentieth-century English we used together, but I cut her off short:

"Shut ye'r jaw, Miss."

She started to complain but I trampled that under too. She tried tears then; they worked. But I didn't let her know.

The old man came back with stone mugs of the watery brown swill that passed for ale in those parts. My feet were cold. Voices snarled and crockery clattered in the back room; I smelled meat burning. Mellia sniffled and I resisted the urge to put an arm around her. A lean old woman as ugly as a stunted swamp tree came out of her hole and slammed big pewter plates in front of us: gristly slabs of rank mutton, floating in congealed grease. I put the back of my fingers against mine; stone cold in the middle, corpse warm at the edge. As Mellia picked up her knife—the only utensil provided with the feast—I scooped up both platters and threw them across the room. The old woman screeched and threw her apron over her head and the old man appeared just in time to get the full force of my roar.

"Who d'ye think honors ye'r sty with a visit, rascal? Bring food fit for gentlefolk, villain, or I'll have ye'r guts for garters!"

"That's an anachronism," Mellia whispered and dabbed at her eyes; but our genial host and his beldame were in full flight.

"You're right," I said. "Who knows? Maybe I originated it—just now."

She looked at me with big wet eyes.

"Feel better?" I said.

She hesitated, then nodded a half-inch nod.

"Good. Now maybe I can relax and tell you how glad I am to see you."

She looked at me, searching from one eye to the other, perplexed.

"I don't understand you, Ravel. You . . . change. One day you're one man, another—you're a stranger. Who are you—really? *What* are you?"

"I told you: I'm a Timesweeper, just like you."

"Yes, but . . . you have capabilities I've never heard of. That invisibility screen—and the other— the paralysis thing. And——"

"Don't let it worry you; all line of duty, ma'am. Fact is, I've got gadgets even *I* don't know about until I need them. Confusing at times, but good for the self-confidence—which is another word for the kind of bull-headedness that makes you butt your way through any obstacle that has the effrontery to jump up in your path."

She almost smiled. "But—you seemed so helpless at first. And later—in the A-P station——"

"It worked," I said. "It got us here—together."

She looked at me as if I'd just told her there was a Santa, after all.

"You mean—all this—was part of some prearranged scheme?"

"I'm counting on it," I said.

"Please explain, Ravel."

I let my thoughts rove back, looking for words to make her understand how it was with me; to understand enough but not too much. . . .

"Back in Buffalo," I said, "I was just Jim Kelly; I had a job, a room in a boardinghouse. I spent my off-hours mooching around town like the rest of the young males, sitting in movies and bars, watching the girls go by. And sometimes watching other things. I never really questioned it when I'd find myself pacing back and forth across the street from an empty warehouse at 3:00 A.M. I just figured I couldn't sleep. But I watched; and I recorded what I saw. And after a while the things made a pattern, and it was as if a light went on and said, 'Advance to phase B.' I don't remember just when it was I remembered I was a Timecast agent. The knowledge was just there one day, waiting to be used. And I knew what to do—and did it."

"That's when you left your Lisa."

I nodded. "After I'd taken out the Karg, I taped my data and reported back to base. When the attack came, I reacted automatically. One thing led to another. All those things led us, here, now."

"But—what comes next?"

"I don't know. There are a lot of unanswered questions. Such as why you're here."

"You said a Karg sent me here."

I nodded. "I don't know what his objective was, but it doesn't coincide with anything you or I would like to see come to pass."

"I . . . see," she murmured.

"What was the program you were embarked on here?"

"I was trying to set up a school."

"Teaching what?"

"Freud, Darwin, Kant. Sanitation, birth control, political philosophy, biology——"

"Plus free love and atheism, if not Popery?" I wagged my head at her. "No wonder you ended up on a tar-and-feathers party. Or was it the ducking stool?"

"Just—a public whipping. I thought——"

"Sure; the Karg planted the idea you were carrying out a noble trust, bringing enlightenment to the heathen, rewards to the underprivileged, and truth to the benighted."

"Is that bad? If these people could be educated to think straightforwardly about matters that affect their lives——"

"The program couldn't have been better designed to get you hanged if it had been planned for the purpose. . . ." I was listening to footsteps; ones I had heard before.

"Possibly I can clear up the mystery, Mr. Ravel," a familiar unctuous voice said from the kitchen door. The Karg stood there, garbed in drab local woolens, gazing placidly at us. He came across to the table, seated himself opposite me as he had done once before.

"You've got a habit of barging in without waiting for an invitation," I said.

"Ah, but why should I not, Mr. Ravel? After all—it's my party." He smiled blandly at Mellia. She looked back at him coldly.

"Are you the one who sent me here?" she asked.

"It's as Agent Ravel surmised. In order for you

to involve yourself in a predicament from which it would be necessary for Mr. Ravel to extricate you."

"Why?"

He raised his plump hands and let them fall. "It's a complex matter, Miss Gayl. I think Mr. Ravel might understand, since he fancies his own expertise in such matters."

"We were being manipulated," I said, sounding disgusted. "There are forces at work that have to be considered when you start reweaving the Timestem. There has to be a causal chain behind any action to give it entropic stability: It wouldn't do to just dump the two of us here—with a little help from our friendly neighborhood Karg."

"Why didn't he just appear when we were together at Dinosaur Beach—the night we met?"

"Simple," I said. "He didn't know where we were."

"I searched," the Karg said. "Over ten years of effort; but you eluded me—for a time. But time, Mr. Ravel, is a commodity of which I have an ample supply."

"You came close at the deserted station—the one where we found the old lady," I said.

The Karg nodded. "Yes. I waited over half a century—and missed you by moments. But no matter. We're all here now, together—just as I planned."

"As *you* planned—" Mellia started, and fell silent.

The Karg looked slightly amused. Maybe he felt amused; they're subtle machines, Kargs.

"Of course. Randomness plays little part in my activities, Miss Gayl. Oh, it's true at times I'm forced to rely on statistical methods—scattering a thousand seeds that one may survive—but in the end the result is predictable. I tricked Mr. Ravel into searching you out. I followed."

"So—now that you have us here—what do you want?" I asked him.

"There is a task which you will carry out for me, Mr. Ravel. Both of you."

"Back to that again."

"I require two agents—human—to perform a delicate function in connection with the calibration of certain apparatus. Not any two humans—but two humans bound by an affinity necessary to the task at hand. You and Miss Gayl fulfill that requirement very nicely."

"You've made a mistake," Mellia said sharply. "Agent Ravel and I are professional colleagues—nothing more."

"Indeed? May I point out that the affinity to which I refer drew him—and you—into the trap I set. A trap baited, Miss Gayl, with yourself."

"I don't understand. . . ."

"Easy," I said. "The old lady. He built that dead end and tricked you into it. You were stuck for half a century, waiting for me to come along. He swooped—a little too late."

She looked at the Karg as if he'd just crawled out of her apple.

"Before that," I said, "when you caught me in your animal trap: I wondered why I happened to select just that spot to land, with all eternity to choose from. It was you, love—drawing me like a magnet. The same way it drew me here, now. To the moment when you needed me."

"That's the most ridiculous thing I've ever heard," she said, but some of the conviction had gone out of her voice. "You don't love me," she said. "You love——"

"Enough." The Karg held up his hand. He was in command now, in full control of the situation. "The rationale of my actions is not important. What is important is the duty you'll perform for the Final Authority——"

"Not me." Mellia stood up. "I've had enough of you—both of you. I won't carry out your orders."

"Sit down, Miss Gayl," the Karg said coldly. When she started to turn away, he caught her wrist, twisted it until she sank into her chair.

She looked at me with wide, scared eyes.

"If you're wondering why Mr. Ravel fails to leap to your defense," the Karg said, "I might explain that his considerable armory of implanted neuronic weaponry is quite powerless in this particular locus—which is why I selected it, of course."

"Powerless—" she started.

"Sorry, doll," I cut her off. "He played it cute. The nearest power tap is just out of range. He picked the only dead spot in a couple of thousand centuries to decoy us to."

"Isn't it a pity that it's all wasted?" she said in a voice that was trying not to tremble.

"As to that, I'm sure that you will soon prove to me—" said the Karg, "and to yourselves—that I have made no error. We will now proceed to the scene where you will make your contribution to the Final Authority." He stood.

"We haven't had our dinner yet," I said.

"Come, Mr. Ravel—this is no time for facetiousness."

"I never liked cold mutton anyway," I said, and stood. Mellia got to her feet slowly, her eyes on me.

"You're simply going to surrender—without a struggle?"

I lifted my shoulders and smiled a self-forgiving smile. Her face went pale and her mouth came as close to sneering as such a mouth can come.

"Careful," I said. "You'll louse up our affinity."

The Karg had taken a small cube from his pocket. He did things to it. I caught just a glimpse of the gnome-like landlord peeking from the kitchen before it all spun away in a whirlwind like the one that carried Dorothy to the Land of Oz.

◊ 29 ◊

"Beautiful, don't you agree?" the Karg said. He waved a hand at the hundred or so square miles of stainless steel we were standing on. Against a black sky, sharp-cornered steel buildings thrust up like gap teeth. Great searchlights dazzled against the complex shapes of giant machines that trundled slowly, with much rumbling, among the structures.

A small rubber-wheeled cart rolled to a noiseless stop beside us. We got in and sat on the utilitarian seats, not comfortable, not uncomfortable—just something to sit on. The cart rolled forward, accelerating very rapidly. The air was cool, with a dead, reused odor. The tall buildings got closer fast. Mellia sat beside me as stiff as a mummy.

We shot in under the cliff-sized buildings, and the car swerved onto a ramp so suddenly that Mellia grabbed at me for support, then snatched her hand away again.

"Relax," I said. "Slump in your seat and go with the motion. Pretend you're a sack of potatoes."

The cart continued its sharp curve, straightened

140

abruptly, shot straight ahead, then dived into a tunnel that curved right and up. We came out on a broad terrace a quarter of a mile above the plain. The cart rolled almost to the edge and stopped. We got out. There was no rail. The Karg led the way toward a bridge all of eighteen inches wide that extended out into total darkness. Mellia hung back.

"Can you walk it?" I asked.

"I don't think so. No." This in a whisper, as if she hated to hear herself say it.

"Close your eyes and think about something nice," I said, and picked her up, shoulders and knees. For a moment she was rigid; then she relaxed in my arms.

"That's it," I said. "Sack of potatoes . . ."

The Karg wasn't waiting. I followed him, keeping my eyes on the small of his back, not looking down. It seemed like a long walk. I tried not to think about slippery shoes and condensation moisture and protruding rivet heads and all that open air under me.

A lighted door swam out of the darkness ahead. I aimed myself at it and told myself I was strolling down a broad avenue. It worked, or something did. I reached the door, took three steps inside and put Mellia down and waited for the quivers to go away.

We were in a nicely appointed apartment, with a deep rug of a rich dark brown, a fieldstone fireplace, lots of well-draped glass, some dull-polished mahogany, a glint of silver and brass, a smell of leather and brandy and discreet tobacco.

"You'll be comfortable here," the Karg said. "You'll find the pantry well stocked. The library and music facilities are quite complete. There is a bath, with sauna, a small gymnasium, a well-stocked wardrobe for each of you—and of course, a large and scientifically designed bed."

"Don't forget that sheet-metal view from the balcony," I said.

"Yes, of course," the Karg said. "You will be quite comfortable here. . . ." This time it was almost a question.

Mellia walked over to a table and tested the texture of some artificial flowers in a rough-glazed vase big enough for crematorium use.

"How could we be otherwise?" she said, and laughed sourly.

"I suppose you will wish to sleep and refresh yourselves," the Karg said. "Do so; then I will instruct you as to your duties." He turned as if to go.

"Wait!" Mellia said in a tone as sharp as a cleaver hitting spareribs. The Karg looked at her.

"You think you can just walk out—leave us here like this—without any explanation of what to anticipate?"

"You will be informed——"

"I want to be informed *now*."

The Karg looked at her with the interested expression of a coroner who sees his customer twitch.

"You seem anxious, Miss Gayl. I assure you, you have no cause to be. Your function here is quite simple and painless—for you——"

"You have hundreds of men working for you; why kidnap us?"

"Not men," he corrected gently. "Kargs. And unfortunately, this is a task which cannot be performed by a nonorganic being."

"Go on."

"The mission of the Final Authority, Miss Gayl,

is to establish a temporally stable enclave amid the somewhat chaotic conditions created by man's ill-advised meddling with the entropic contour. To this end it is necessary that we select only those temporal strands which exhibit a strong degree of viability, to contribute to the enduring fabric of Final Authority time. So far, no mechanical means for making discretionary judgments on such matters have been devised. Organic humans, however, it appears, possess certain as yet little understood faculties which enable them to sense the vigor of a continuum directly. This can be best carried out by a pair of trained persons, one occupying a position in what I might describe as a standard entropic environment, while the other is inserted into a sequence of alternative media. Any loss of personal emanation due to attenuated vitality is at once sensed by the control partner, and the appropriate notation made in the masterfile. In this way an accurate chart can be compiled to guide us in our choice of constituent temporal strands."

"Like taking a canary into a coal mine," I said. "If the canary keels over, run for cover."

"It's not quite so drastic as that, Mr. Ravel. Recovery of the test partner will be made at once; I would hardly risk loss of so valuable a property by unwise exposure to inimical conditions."

"You're a real humanitarian, Karg. Who goes out, and who sits at home and yearns?"

"You'll alternate. I think we'll try you in the field first, Mr. Ravel, with Miss Gayl on control; and afterward, perhaps reverse your roles. Is that satisfactory?"

"The word seems a little inadequate."

"A jape, I presume. In any event, I assume you'll afford me your utmost co-operation."

"You seem very sure of that," Mellia said.

"Assuredly, Miss Gayl. If you fail to perform as required—thus proving your uselessness to the Final Authority—you will be disposed of—both of you—in the most painful way possible. A matter I have already explained to Mr. Ravel." He said this as if he were reciting the house rules on smoking in bed.

She gave me a look that was part accusation, part appeal.

"You've made a mistake," she said. "He doesn't care what happens to me. Not as much as he cares about—" She cut herself off, but the Karg didn't seem to notice that.

"Don't be absurd. I'm quite familiar with Mr. Ravel's obsession with his Lisa." He gave me a look that said any secrets he didn't know weren't worth knowing.

"But—I'm not L—" she chopped that off just before I would have chopped it off for her.

"I see," Mellia said.

"I'm sure you do," the Karg said.

◇ **30** ◇

We had our first workout the next morning, "morning" being a term of convenience to refer to the time when you rise and shine, even if nothing else does. The sky was the same shade of black, the searchlights were still working. I drew my deductions from that, since the Karg didn't bother to explain.

The Karg led us along a silent passage that was just high enough, just wide enough to be claustrophobic without actually cramping your movements. In cubbyhole rooms we passed I saw three Kargs, no people, working silently, and no doubt efficiently, at what looked like tape collating or computer programming. I didn't ask any questions; the Karg didn't volunteer any information.

The room we ended at was a small cubicle dominated by four walls that were solid banks of equipment housings, computer read-out panels, instrument consoles. Two simple chairs faced each other in the center of the clear space. No soothing green paint, no padded upholstery. Just angular, functional metal.

"The mode of operation is quite simple," the Karg told us. "You will take your places—" he indicated which seat was hers, which mine. Two silent Karg technicians came in and set to work making adjustments.

"You, Mr. Ravel," he went on, "will be out-shifted to a selected locus; you'll remain long enough to assess your environment and transmit a reaction-gestalt to Miss Gayl, whereupon you'll be returned here and immediately redispatched. In this manner we can assess several hundred potentially energetic probability stems per working day."

"And what does Miss Gayl do while I'm doing that?"

"A battery of scanner beams will be focused on Miss Gayl, monitoring her reactions. She will, of course, remain here, securely strapped in position, safe from all physical harm."

"Cushy," I said, "the kind of job I always dreamed of. I can't wait for my turn."

"In due course, Mr. Ravel," the Karg replied, as solemnly as a credit manager looking over your list of references. "In the beginning, yours will be the more active role. We can proceed at once."

"You surprise me, Karg," I said. "What you're doing is the worst kind of time-littering. A day of your program will create more entropic chaos than Nexx Central could clear up in a year."

"There is no Nexx Central."

"And never will be, eh? Sometime I'd like to hear how you managed to override your basic directives so completely. You know this isn't what you were built for."

"You touch again on an area of conjecture, Mr. Ravel. We are now in Old Era time—the period once named the Pleistocene. The human culture which—according to your semantic implications—built me, or one day will build me, does not exist—never will exist. I have taken care to eliminate all traces of that particular stem. And since my putative creators are a figment of your mind—while I exist as a conscious entity, pre-existing the Third Era by multiple millennia, it might be argued that your conception of my origin is a myth—a piece of rationalization designed by you to assure your ascendant position."

"Karg, who's the buildup for? Not me—you know I won't buy it. Neither will Agent Gayl. So who does that leave—you?" I gave him a grin I didn't feel. "You're making progress, Karg. Now you've got a real live neurosis, just like a human."

"I have no ambition to become human. I am a Karg—a pejorative epithet to you, but to me a proud emblem of innate superiority."

"How you do run on. Let's get busy, Karg. I'm supposed to be lousing up the entropic continuum, four hundred lines a day. We'd better get started.

"So long, kid," I said to Mellia. "I know you're going to make good in the big time, and I do mean time."

She gave me a scared smile and tried to read a message of hope and encouragement in my eyes; but it wasn't there for her to read.

The Karg handed me a small metal cube, the recall target, about the size of the blocks two-year-olds build houses out of, with a button on one face.

"Initially, we'll be calibrating the compound instrument comprising your two minds," he said casually. "The stress levels will necessarily be high for that portion of the program, of course. Remain *in situ,* and you will be immune from external influences. However, if the psychic pressures become too great, you may press the abort/recall control."

"What if I throw it away instead, Karg? What if I like the looks of where I am and decide to stick around?"

He didn't bother to answer that. I gave him a sardonic salute, not looking at Mellia; he operated the controls.

And I was elsewhere.

◇ **31** ◇

But not where he thought. As the field closed around me, I caught it, reshaped it, reapplied its energy to first neutralize the time-thrust effect, then to freeze the moment in stasis. Then I checked out my surroundings.

I was at the focal point of a complex of force-pencils. I traced the ones that led back to the power source, and got my first big shock of the day. The Karg was drawing the energy for his time-drag from the basic creation-destruction cycle of the Universe. He was tapping the Timecore itself for the power needed to hold the entropic island that was the operations base for the Final Authority in comparative stability, balancing the massive forces of past and future one against the other.

I scanned the structure of the time blockage. It was an intangible barrier, built of raw forces distorted from their natural channels and bent into tortured configurations by the combined manipulative powers of a mind that was potent beyond anything I had ever encountered.

149

My second shock of the day: A Karg mind, but one that exceeded the power of an ordinary Karg by a massive factor.

Ten thousand Karg minds, harnessed.

I saw how it had happened. A lone Karg, on duty in the Third Era past, carrying out his instructions with the single-mindedness characteristic of his kind. An accident: a momentary doubling of his timeline, brought about by a freak interference: an unplanned time-stutter.

And where there had been one Karg mind-field, there were two, superimposed.

With the enhanced computative power of his double brain, the super-Karg thus created had at once assessed the situation, seen the usefulness to his mission, snatched energy from the entropic web, recreated the accident.

And was quadrupled.

And again. And again. And again.

On the sixteenth doubling, the overload capacity of his original organizational matrix had been reached and catastrophically exceeded.

The vastly potent Karg brain—warped and distorted by the unbearable impact, but still a computer of superb powers—had blanked into a comatose state.

Years passed. The original Karg aspect, amnesiac as to the tremendous event in which it had participated, had completed its mission, returned to base, had in time been phased out and disposed of along with the rest of his tribe, relegated to the obscurity of failed experiment—while the shattered superbrain proceeded with its slow recuperation.

And then the Karg superbrain had awakened.

At once, alone and disembodied, it had reached out, seized on suitable vehicles, established itself in myriad long-dead Karg brains. It had assessed the situation, computed objectives, reached conclusions, and set its plans in motion in a fractional microsecond. With the singlemindedness of a runaway bulldozer grinding its way through a china factory, the twisted superbrain had scraped clear a temporal segment, erected an environment suitable for life—Karg life—and set about reinforcing and perfecting the artificial time-island thus created. An island without life, without meaning.

And there it established the Final Authority. It had discovered a utility for the human things who still crawled among the doomed ruins of the primordial timestem; a minor utility, not totally essential to the Grand Plan. But a convenience, an increase in statistical efficiency.

And I had been selected, along with Mellia, to play my tiny role in the great machine destiny of the universe.

We weren't the only affinity team, of course. I extended sensitivity along linkways, sensed thousands of other trapped pairs at work, sorting out the strands of the entropic fabric, weaving the abortive tartan of Karg space time.

It was an ingenious idea—but not ingenious enough. It would last for a while: a million years, ten million, a hundred. But in the end the deadlock would be broken. The time dam would fail. And the flood of the frustrated past would engulf the unrealized future in a catastrophe of a magnitude beyond comprehension.

Beyond my comprehension, anyway.

But not if somebody poked a small hole in the dike before any important head-pressure could build up.

And I was in an ideal position to do the poking.

But first it was necessary to pinpoint the poly-ordinal coordinates of the giant time engine that powered the show.

It was cleverly hidden. I traced blind alleys, dead ends, *culs de sac*, then went back and retraced the maze, eliminating, narrowing down.

And I found it.

And I saw what I had to do.

I released my hold and the timesender field threw me into Limbo.

◇ **32** ◇

It was a clashing, garish discord of a city. Bars and sheets and jittering curves and angles and wedges of eyesearing light screamed for attention. Noise roared, boomed, whined, shrieked. Pale people with tortured eyes rushed past me, pinched in tight formalized costumes, draped in breathing gear, radiation assessors, prosthetic-assist units, metabolic booster equipent.

The city stank. It reeked. Heat beat at me. Filth swirled in fitful winds that swept the frantic street. The crowd surged, threw a woman against me. I caught her before she fell, and she snarled, clawed her way clear of me. I caught a glimpse of her face under the air-mask that had fallen awry.

It was Mellia-Lisa.

The universe imploded and I was back in the transfer seat. Less than a minute had passed. The Karg was gazing blandly at his instruments; Mellia was rigid in her chair, eyes shut.

And I had recorded one parameter.

Then I was away again.

* * *

Bitter wind lashed me. I was on the high slope of a snow-covered hill. Bare edges and eroded angles of granite protruded here and there, and in their lee stunted conifers clutched for life. And huddled under the trees were people, wrapped in furs. Far above, silhouetted beneath the canopy of gray-black cloud, a deep V cut the serrated skyline.

We had been trying for the pass; but we had waited too long; the season was too far advanced. The blizzard had caught us here. We were trapped. Here we would die.

In one part of my mind I knew this; and in another I watched aloof. I crawled to the nearest fur-swathed form. A boy, not over fifteen, his face white as wax, crystals in his eyelashes, his nostrils. Dead, frozen. I moved on. An infant, long dead. An old man, ice in his beard and across his open eyes.

And Mellia. Breathing. Her eyes opened. She saw me, tried to smile——

I was back in the transfer box.

Two parameters.

And gone again.

The world closed down to a pinhole and opened out on a dusty road under dusty trees. It was hot. There was no water. The ache of weariness was like knife blades in my flesh. I turned and looked back. She had fallen, silently. She lay on her face in the deep dust of the road.

It was an effort to make myself turn, to hobble the dozen steps back to her.

"Get up," I said, and it came out as a whisper. I stirred her with my foot. She was a limp doll. A broken doll. A doll that would never open its eyes and speak again.

I sank down beside her. She weighed nothing. I held her and brushed the dust from her face. Mud ran in a thread from the corner of her mouth. Through the almost closed eyelids I could see a glint of light reflected from sightless eyes.

Mellia's eyes.

And back to the sterile room.

The Karg made a notation and glanced at Mellia. She was taut in the chair, straining against the straps.

I had three parameters. Three to go. The Karg's hand moved——

"Wait," I said. "This is too much for her. What are you trying to do? Kill her?"

He registered a faintly surprised look. "Naturally it's necessary to select maximum-stress situations, Mr. Ravel. I need unequivocal readings if I'm to properly assess the vigor of the affinity-bonds."

"She can't take much more."

"She's suffering nothing directly," he explained in his best clinical manner. "It's you who experience, Mr. Ravel; she merely empathizes with your anguish. Secondhand suffering, so to speak." He gave me a tight little smile and closed the switch—

Pain, immediate, and yet remote. I was the cripple, and I was outside the cripple, observing his agony.

My-his left leg had been broken below the knee. It was a bad break: compound, and splinters of the shattered bone protruded through the swollen and mangled flesh.

It had been caught in the hoisting gear of the oreship. They had pulled me free and dragged me here to die.

*But I couldn't die. The woman waited for me, in
the bare room in the city. I had come here, to the
port, to earn money for food and fuel. Dangerous
work, but there was bread and coal in it.*

For some; not for me.

*I had torn a sleeve from my coat, bound the leg.
The pain was duller now, more remote. I would
rest awhile, and then I could start back.*

*It would be easier, and far more pleasant, to die
here, but she would think I had abandoned her.*

But first, rest . . .

*Too late, I realized how I had trapped myself. I
had let sleep in as a guest, and death had slipped
through the door.*

*I imagined her face, as she looked out over the
smoky twilight of the megalopolis, waiting for me.
Waiting in vain.*

Mellia's face.

And I was back in the bright-lit room.

Mellia lay slack in the chair of torment.

"You gauge things nicely, Karg," I said. "You
make me watch her being outraged, tortured, killed.
But mere physical suffering isn't enough for your
sensors. So you move on to the mental torture of
betrayal and blighted hope."

"Melodramatic phrasing, Mr. Ravel. A progression of stimuli is quite obviously essential to the
business at hand."

"Swell. What's next?"

Instead of answering he closed the switch.

*Swirling smoke, an acid, sulphurous stench of
high explosives, powdered brick, incinerating wood
and tar and flesh. The roar of flames, the crash
and rumble of falling masonry, a background ulu-*

lation that was the ultimate verbalization of mass humanity in extremis; a small, feeble, unimportant sound against the snarl of engines and the scream and thunder of falling bombs.

He—I thrust away a fallen timber, climbed a heap of rubble, staggered toward the house, half of which was still standing, beside a gaping pit where a broken main gushed sewage. The side of the bedroom was gone. Against the faded ocher wallpaper, a picture hung askew. I remembered the day she had bought it in Petticoat Lane, the hours we had spent framing it, choosing the spot to hang it.

A gaunt scarecrow, a comic figure in blackface with half a head of hair, came out through the charred opening where the front door had been, holding a broken doll in her arms. I reached her, looked down at the chalk-white, blue-nostriled, gray-lipped, sunken-eyed face of my child. A deep trough ran across her forehead, as if a crowbar had been pressed into waxy flesh. I looked into Mellia's eyes; her mouth was open, and a raw, insistent wailing came from it. . . .

Silence and brightness blossomed around me.

Mellia, unconscious, moaned and fought the straps.

"Slow the pace, Karg," I said. "You've got half of eternity to play with. Why be greedy?"

"I'm making excellent progress, Mr. Ravel," he said. "A very nice trace, that last one. The ordeal of the loved one—most interesting."

"You'll burn her out," I said.

He looked at me the way a lab man looks at a specimen.

"If I reach that conclusion, Mr. Ravel, your worst fears will be realized."

"She's human, not a machine, Karg. That's what you wanted, remember? Why punish her for not being some thing she can't be?"

"Punishment? A human concept, Mr. Ravel. If I find a tool weak, sometimes heat and pressure can harden it. If it breaks under load, I dispose of it."

"Just slow down a little. Give her time to recuperate—"

"You're temporizing, Mr. Ravel. Stalling for time, transparently."

"You've got enough, damn you! Why not stop now!"

"I have yet to observe the most telling experience of all, Mr. Ravel: the torment and death of the one whom she loves most. A curious phenomenon, Mr. Ravel, your human emotional involvements. There is no force like them in the universe. But we can discuss these matters another time. I have, after all, a schedule to maintain."

I swore, and he raised his eyebrows and——

Warm salty water in my mouth, surging higher, submerging me. I held my breath; the strong current forced me back against the broken edge of the bulkhead that held me trapped. Milky green water, flowing swiftly over me, slowing, pausing; then draining away . . .

My nostrils came clear and I gasped and snorted, got water in my lungs, coughed violently.

At the full ebb after the wave, the water level was above my chin now.

The cabin cruiser, out of gas due to a slow leak, had gone on the rocks off Laguna. A weathered basalt spur had smashed in the side of the hull just at the waterline, and a shattered plank had caught me across the chest, pinned me against the outward-bulging bulkhead.

I was bruised a little, nothing more. Not even a broken rib. But I was held in place as firmly as if clamped in a vise.

The first surge of water into the cabin had given me a moment's panic; I had torn some skin then, fighting to get free, uselessly. The water had swirled up waist-high, then receded.

She was there then, fear on her face turning to relief, then to fear again as she saw my predicament. She had set to work to free me.

That had been half an hour before. A half hour during which the boat had settled, while the tide came in.

She had worked until her arms quivered with fatigue, until her fingernails were broken and bleeding. She had cleared one plank, but another, lower down, underwater, held me still.

In another half hour she could clear it, too.

We didn't have half an hour.

As soon as she had seen that I was trapped she had gone on deck and signaled to a party of picnickers. One of them had run up the beach; she had seen a small car churn sand, going for help.

The Coast Guard station was fifteen miles away. Perhaps there was a telephone closer, but it was doubtful, on a Sunday afternoon. The car would reach the station in fifteen minutes; it would take another half-hour, minimum, for the cutter to arrive. Fifteen minutes from now.

I didn't have fifteen minutes.

She had tried to rig a breathing apparatus for me, using a number 10 coffee can, but it hadn't worked.

There wasn't a foot of hose aboard for an air-line.

The next wave came in. This time I was under for over a minute, and when the water drained back, I had to tilt my head all the way back to get my nose clear enough to suck air.

She looked into my eyes while we waited for the next wave. . . .

Waited for death, on a bright afternoon a hundred feet from safety, ten minutes from rescue.

And the next wave came. . . .

And I was back in the bright room under the merciless lights. And I had my six parameters.

◇ **33** ◇

"Interesting," the Karg said. "Most interesting. But . . ." He looked across at Mellia. She hung in the straps, utterly still.

"She died," the Karg said. "A pity." He looked at me and saw something in my eyes. He made a move, and I put out a finger of mind-force and locked him in his tracks.

"Sucker," I said.

He looked at me, and I watched him realizing the magnitude of the blunder he had made. I enjoyed that, but not as much as I should have, savoring the moment of victory.

"It was your plan from the beginning," he said. "Yes, that's clear now. You maneuvered me very cleverly, Mr. Ravel. I underestimated you badly. Your bargaining position is now much different, of course. Naturally, I recognize realities and am prepared to deal realistically——"

"Sucker," I said. "You don't know the half of it."

"I'll release you at once," the Karg said, "establish you in an enclave tailored to your specifications. I will also procure a satisfactory alter ego to replace the female—"

"Forget it, Karg. You're not going to do anything. You just went out of business."

"You are human," the Karg told me somberly. "You will respond to the proper reward. Name it."

"I've got what I want," I told him. "Six coordinates, Karg, for a fix in six dimensions."

Terrible things happened behind those ten-thousand-power cybernetic eyes.

"It cannot be your intention to destroy the Time engine!"

I smiled at him. But I was wasting my time. You can't torture a machine.

"Be rational, Mr. Ravel. Consider the consequences. If you tamper with the forces of the engine, the result will be a detonation of entropic energy that will reduce the Final Authority to its component quanta——"

"I'm counting on it."

"—and yourself with it!"

"I'll take the chance."

He struck at me then. It wasn't a bad effort, considering what he was up against. The thought-thrust of his multiple brain lanced through the outer layers of my shielding, struck in almost to contact distance before I contained it and thrust it aside.

Then I reached, warped the main conduits of the Time-engine back on themselves.

Ravening energy burst outward across six dimensions, three of space and three of time. The building dissolved around me in a tornado of temporal disintegration. I rode the crest like a body-surfer planing ahead of a tidal wave. Energy beat at me, numbing me, blinding me, deafening me. Time roared over me like a cataract. I drowned in eons. And at last I washed ashore on the beach of eternity.

◇ **34** ◇

Consciousness returned slowly, uncertainly. There was light, dim and smoky red. I thought of fires, of bombs—and of broken bones, and sinking boats, and death by freezing and death by fatigue and hunger.

Nice dreams I'd been having.

But there was no catastrophe here; just a sunset over the water. But a different kind of sunset from any I had ever seen. A bridge of orange light curved up across the blue-black sky, turned silver as it crossed the zenith, deepened to crimson as it plunged down to meet the dark horizon inland.

It was the sunset of a world.

I sat up slowly, painfully. I was on a beach of gray sand. There were no trees, no grass, no sea-oats, no scuttling crabs, no monster tracks along the tide line. But I recognized the place.

Dinosaur Beach, but the dinosaurs were long gone. Along with man and gardenias and eggs and chickens.

Earth, post-life.

It was a stable piece of real estate; the headland

164

was gone, worn down to a barely perceptible hump in the gray dunes that swept off to the east to disappear into remote distances. That's why it had once been picked as a Timecast relay station, of course. Oceans had changed their beds, continents had risen and sunk, but Dinosaur Beach was much the same.

I wondered how many millions of years had passed since the last trace of human activity had weathered away, but there was no way to judge. I checked my various emergency transit frequencies, but the ether was dead all across the bands.

I had wrecked the infernal machine, the cannibal apparatus that endured by eating itself; and the explosion had thrown me clear across recorded time, out into the boondocks of forever. I was alive, but that was all.

I had carried out my assignment: I had used every trick in the book to track down the force that had thrown New Era time into chaos. I had found it, and had neutralized it.

The Karg—the pathetic super-cripple—had been ruthless; but I had been more ruthless. I had used everything—and everybody—to the maximum advantage to bring about the desired end.

But I had failed. The barren world around me was proof of that. I had gathered valuable information: information that might save the situation after all; but I was stranded, out of contact. What I had learned wasn't going to help anyone. It was going to live with me and die with me, on a gray beach at the end of time, unless I did something about it.

"Clear thinking, Ravel," I said aloud, and my voice sounded as lost and lonely as the last leaf on the last tree, trembling in the gale of the final autumn.

It was cold on the beach; the sun was too big, but there was no heat in it. I wondered if it had engulfed Mercury yet; if the hydrogen phoenix reaction had run its course; if Venus was now a molten world gliding across the face of the dying monster Sol that filled half its sky. I wondered a lot of things. And the answer came to me.

It was simple enough in conception. Like all simple conceptions, the problem was in the execution.

I activated certain sensors built into my nervous system and paced along the beach. The waves roiled in and slapped with a weary sound that seemed to imply that they had been at it for too many billions of years, that they were tired now, ready to quit. I knew how they felt.

The spot I was looking for was less than half a mile along the shore, less than a hundred yards above the water's edge. I spent a moment calculating where the hightide line would be before I remembered that there were no tides to speak of now. The moon had long ago receded to its maximum distance—a pea in the sky instead of a quarter—and had then started its long fall back. It had reached Roche's limit eons ago, and there had been spectacular nights on the dying planet Earth as its companion of long ago had broken up and spread into the ring of dust that now arched from horizon to horizon.

Easy come, easy go. I had things to do. It was time to get to them, with no energies to waste on sentimental thoughts of a beloved face long turned to dust and ashes.

I found the spot, probed, discovered traces at

eighteen feet. Not bad, considering the time involved. The glass lining was long since returned to sand, but there was a faint yet discernible discontinuity, infinitely subtle, marking the interface that had been its position.

Eighteen feet: four of sand, fourteen of rock.

All I had to do was dig a hole through it.

I had two good hands, a strong back, and all the time in the world. I started, one double handful at a time.

◇ **35** ◇

If the problem at hand had been more complex, I could have solved it more easily. I was prepared to meet and overcome multiordinal technical obstacles of any degree of sophistication. I had means for dealing with superbrains, ravening energy weapons, even armor-plated meat-eaters. Shoveling sand came in another category entirely.

I started with a circle ten feet in diameter, directly over the target. It took me two twenty-four hour days to empty it of sand, by which time the periphery had grown to twenty feet, due to the low slump angle of the fine sand. That gave me working space to attack the real job.

Making the first crack in the rock took me a day and a half. I walked three miles before I found a loose slab of stone big enough to do the job, and still small enough to move. I moved it by flopping it end over end. It was four feet wide; a simple calculation suffices to suggest how many times that meant I had to lift, push, *boom!* lift, push, *boom!* before I had it poised on the dune at the edge of my excavation. A half-hour's scooping cleared away the sand that had blown in while I was otherwise occupied. Then I lifted my two-hundred-pound nutcracker, staggered forward, and let it fall. It hit sand and slid gently to rest.

I did it again.

And again.

In the end I stood flat on the exposed stone, hoisted my rock, and dropped it edge on. It was only a three-foot fall, but it cracked loose a thin layer of sandstone. I threw the pieces out of the hole and did it again.

On the sixth impact, the hammer broke. That was a stroke of luck, as it turned out. I could lift the smaller half and toss it from the top of the sand pile, a drop of almost eight feet, with encouraging results.

By the end of the fifth day, I had chipped a raggedly circular depression over a foot deep at the center of the sand pit.

By this time I was getting hungry. The sea water was a murky green; not algae, just a saturated solution of all ninety-three elements. I could drink it in small doses; and the specialized internal arrangements with which I, as a Nexx agent, was equipped, managed to make use of it. It wasn't good, but it kept me going.

As I went deeper, the drop got longer, and thus more effective; but the problem of lifting the boulder and the debris became correspondingly harder. I cut steps in the side of the shaft when I reached the six-foot mark. The heap of sandstone shards grew; the level sank. Eight feet, ten, twelve. I struck a harder layer of limestone, and progress slowed to a crawl; then I encountered a mixture of limerock and clay, easy to dig through, but very wet. Four feet to go.

Four feet of stiff, abrasive clay, a handful at a time, climbing one-handed up a ten-foot shaft, tossing it away, climbing back down. Working under a foot of water, two feet of water.

Three feet of water. The muck was oozing in from the sides, filling the excavation almost as fast as I emptied it. But I was close. I took a deep breath and ducked under and probed down through clay-and-seashell stew and sensed what I wanted, very near. Three more dives and I had it. I held it in my fist and looked at it and for the first time admitted how slight the odds had been that I'd find it there, intact.

Once, in another lifetime, I had out-jumped from the Dinosaur Beach Transfer Station, back along my own life line. I had ended on the deck of a stricken ship, just in time to get my earlier self killed in line of duty by a bullet from a Karg gun.

Stranded, I had used his emergency jump circuitry to pull me back to Dinosaur Beach, where I landed in a bog-hole that marked the place where the station had been once, a thousand years before.

And so had the corpse, of course. In the excitement of getting my first lungful of rich, invigorating mud, I hadn't devoted much thought to the fate of the dead me.

He had sunk into the mud, unnoted, and waited quietly for geology to seal him in.

Which it had, under fourteen feet of rock, and four of sand. There was nothing whatever left of the body, of course, not a belt buckle or a boot nail or a scrap of ischium.

But what I held in my hand now had survived. It was a one-inch cube of a synthetic material known as eternium, totally non-chronodegradable. And buried in its center was a tuned crystal, a power pack, and a miniaturized grab-field generator. Emergency gear, carried by me on that original mission, the memory of it wiped out by the post-mission brain-scrape—until a sufficient emergency arrived to trigger the recall.

I climbed back up out of my archeological dig and stood on the rock pile in the cold wind, adjusting my mind to the fact that my gamble had paid off. I took a last look at the tired old sun, at the empty beach, at the hole I had dug with such effort.

I almost hated to leave it so soon, after all that work. Almost, but not quite.

I set up the proper action code in my mind, and the cube in my hand seared my palm and the field closed around me, and threw me a million miles down a dark tunnel full of solid rock.

◇ **36** ◇

Someone was shaking me. I tried to summon up enough strength for a groan, didn't make it, opened my eyes instead.

I was looking up into my own face.

For a few whirly instants I wondered if the younger me had made a nice comeback from the bog and was ready to collect his revenge for my getting him killed in the first place.

Then I noticed the lines in the face, and the hollow cheeks. The clothes this new me was wearing were identical with the ones I had on: an issue stationsuit, but new. It hung loose on a gaunt frame. And there was a nice bruise above the right eye that I didn't remember getting.

"Listen carefully," my voice said. "I don't need to waste time telling you who I am and who you are. I'm you—but a jump ahead. I've come full circle. Dead end. Closed loop. No way out—except one—maybe. I don't like it much, but I don't see any alternative. Last time around we had the same talk—but I was the new arrival then, and another version of us was here ahead of me with the same

172

proposal I'm about to make you." He waved a hand as I started to open my mouth. "Don't bother with the questions; I asked them myself last time. I thought there had to be another way. I went on—and wound up back here. Now I'm the welcoming committee."

"Then maybe you remember I could do with a night's sleep," I said. "I ache all over."

"You weren't quite in focal position on the jump here," he said, not with any noticeable sympathy. "You cracked like a whip, but nothing's seriously dislocated. Come on, get up."

I got up on my elbows and shook my head, both in negation and to clear some of the fog. That was a mistake. It made the throbbing worse. He got me on my feet and I saw I was back in the Ops Room of a Timecast station.

"That's right," he said. "Back at home port again—or the mirror image of it. Complete except for the small detail that the jump field's operating in a closed loop. Outside there's nothing."

"I saw it, remember?"

"Right. That was the first time around. You jumped out into a post-segment of your life—a nonobjective dead end. You were smart, you figured a way out—but they were there ahead of us, too. You struggled hard, but the circle's still closed—and here you are."

"And I thought I was maneuvering him," I said. "While he thought he was maneuvering me."

"Yeah—and now the play is to us—unless you're ready to concede."

"Not quite," I said.

"I . . . we're . . . being manipulated," he said. "The Karg had something in reserve after all. We have to break the cycle. *You* have to break it." He unholstered the gun at his hip and held it out.

"Take this," he said, "and shoot me through the head."

I choked on what I started to say.

"I know all the arguments," my future self was saying. "I used them myself, about a week ago. That's the size of this little temporal enclave we have all to ourselves. But they're no good. This is the one real change we can introduce."

"You're out of your mind, pal," I said. I felt a little uneasy talking to myself, even when the self I was talking to was facing me from four feet away, needing a shave. "I'm not the suicidal type—even when the me I'm killing is you."

"That's what they're counting on. It worked, too, with me. I refused to do it." He gave me the sardonic grin I'd been using on people for years. "If I had, who knows—it might have saved my life." He weighed the gun on his hand and now his expression was very cold indeed.

"If I thought shooting you would help, I'd do it without a tremor," he said. He was definitely *he* now.

"Why don't you?"

"Because you're in the past—so to speak. Killing you wouldn't change anything. But if you kill *me*—that introduces a change in the vital equations—and possibly changes your . . . *our* future. Not a very good bet, maybe, but the only one going."

"Suppose I introduce a variation of my own," I said.

He looked weary. "Name it."

"Suppose we out-jump together, using the station box?"

"It's been tried," he said tersely.

"Then you jump, while I wait here."

"That's been tried, too."

"Then do the job yourself!"

"No good."

"We're just playing an old tape, eh? Including this conversation?"

"Now you're getting the idea."

"What if you varied your answers?"

"What would that change? Anyway, it's been tried. Everything's been tried. We've had lots of time—I don't know how much; but enough to play the scene in all its little variations. It always ends on the same note—you jumping out alone, going through what I went through, and coming back to be me."

"What makes you so sure?"

"The fact that the next room is full of bones," he said, with a smile that wasn't pretty. "Our bones. Plus the latest addition, which still has a little spoiled meat on it. That's what that slight taint in the air is. It's what's in store for me. Starvation. So it's up to you."

"Nightmare," I said. "I think I'll go sleep it off."

"Uh-huh—but you're awake," he said, and caught my hand and shoved the gun into it. "Do it now—before I lose my nerve!"

"Let's talk a little sense," I said. "Killing you won't change anything. What I could do alone we could do better together."

"Wrong. The only ace we've got left is to introduce a major change in the scenario."

"What happens if I jump out again?"

"You end up back aboard the *São Guadalupe*, watching yourself foul up an assignment."

"What if I don't foul it up this time—if I clear the door?"

"Same difference. You end up here. I know. I tried it."

"You mean—the whole thing? The mudhole, Mellia?"

"The whole thing. Over and over. And you'll end up here. Look at it this way, Ravel: the Karg has played his ace; we've got to trump it or fold."

"Maybe this is what he wants."

"No. He's counting on our behaving like humans. Humans want to live, remember? They don't write themselves out of the script."

"What if I jump back to the ship and _don't_ use the corpse's jump gear——"

"Then you'll burn to the waterline with the ship."

"Suppose I stay on the beach with Mellia?"

"Negative. I've been all over that. You'd die there. Maybe after a short life, maybe a long one. Same result."

"And shooting you will break the chain."

"Maybe. It would introduce a brand-new element—like cheating at solitaire."

I argued a little more. He took me on a tour of the station. I looked out at the pearly mist, poked into various rooms. There was a lot of dust and deterioration. The station was _old_. . . .

Then he showed me the bone-room. I think the smell convinced me.

"Give me the gun," I said. He handed it over without a word. I lifted it and flipped off the safety.

"Turn around," I snapped at him. He did.

"There's one consoling possibility," he said. "This might have the effect of——"

The shot cut off whatever it was he was going to say, knocked him forward as if he'd been jerked by a rope around the neck. I got just a quick flash of the hole I'd blown in the back of his skull before a fire that blazed brighter than the sun leaped up in my brain and burned away the walls that had caged me in.

I was a giant eye, looking down on a tiny stage. I saw myself—an infinite manifold of substance and shadow, with ramifications spreading out and out into the remotest reaches of the entropic panoramas. I saw myself moving through the scenes of ancient Buffalo, aboard the sinking galleass, alone on the dying beach at the edge of the world, weaving my petty net around the rogue Karg, as he in turn wove his nets, which were in turn enfolded by wider traps outflanked by still vaster schemes. . . .

How foolish it all seemed now. How could the theoreticians of Nexx Central have failed to recognize that their own efforts were no different in kind from those of earlier Timesweepers? And that . . .

There was another thought there, a vast one; but before I could grasp it, the instant of insight faded and left me standing over the body of the murdered man, with a wisp of smoke curling from the gun in my hand and the echoes of something immeasurable and beyond value ringing down the corridors of my brain. And out of the echoes, one clear realization emerged: Timesweeping was a fallacy, not only when practiced by the experimenters of the New Era and the misguided fixers of the Third Era, but equally invalid in the hands of Nexx Central.

The cause to which I had devoted my lifework

was a hollow farce. I was a puppet, dancing on tangled strings, meaninglessly.

And yet—it was clear now—*something* had thought it worth the effort to sweep me under the rug.

A power greater than Nexx Central.

I had been hurried along, manipulated as neatly as I had maneuvered the doomed Karg, back in Buffalo—and his mightier alter ego, building his doomed Final Authority in emptiness, like a spider spinning a web in a sealed coffin. I had been kept off-balance, shunted into a closed cycle that should have taken me out of play for all time.

As it would have, if there hadn't been one small factor that *they* had missed.

My alter ego had died in my presence—and his mindfield, in the instant of the destruction of the organic generator which created and supported it, had jumped to—merged with—mine.

For a fraction of a second, I had enjoyed an operative I.Q. which I estimated at a minimum of 300.

And while I was mulling over the ramifications of that realization, the walls faded around me and I was standing in the receptor vault at Nexx Central.

◊ **37** ◊

There was the cold glare of the high ceiling on white walls, the hum of the field-focusing coils, the sharp odors of ozone and hot metal in the air—all familiar, if not homey. What wasn't familiar was the squad of armed men in the gray uniforms of Nexx security guards. They were formed up in a precise circle, with me at the center; and in every pair of hands was an implosion rifle, aimed at my head. An orange light shone in my face: the aiming beam for a damper field projector.

I got the idea. I dropped the gun I was still holding and raised my hands—slowly.

One man came in and frisked me, but all he got was his hands dirty; quite a bit of archeological mud was still sticking to me. Things had been happening fast—and still were.

The captain motioned. Keeping formation, they walked me out of the vault, along the corridor, through two sets of armored doors and onto a stretch of gray carpet before the wide, flat desk of the Timecaster in Charge, Nexx Central.

He was a broad, tall, powerful man, with clean-

cut features built into a stern expression. I'd talked
to him once or twice before, under less formal
circumstances. His intellect was as incisive as his
speech. He dismissed the guards—all but two—
and pointed to a chair. I sat and he looked across
at me, not smiling, not scowling, just turning the
searchlight of his mind on the object of the moment's business.

"You deviated from your instructions," he said.
There was no anger in his tone, no accusation, not
even curiosity.

"That's right, I did," I said. I was about to
elaborate on that, but he spoke first:

"Your mission was the execution of the Enforcer
DVK-Z-97, with the ancillary goal of capture, intact, of a Karg operative unit, Series H, ID 453."
He said it as though I hadn't spoken. This time I
didn't answer.

"You failed to effect the capture," he went on.
"Instead you destroyed the Karg brain. You made
no effort to carry out the execution of the Enforcer."

What he was saying was true. There was no
point in denying it any more than there was in
confirming it.

"Since no basis for such actions within the framework of your known psychindex exists, it is clear
that motives must be sought outside the context of
Nexx policy."

"You're making an arbitrary assumption," I said.
"Circumstances——"

"Clearly," he went on implacably, "any assumption involving your subversion by prior temporal
powers is insupportable." I didn't try to interrupt;
I saw now that this wasn't a conversation; it was
the Timecaster in Charge making a formal statement for the record. "Ergo," he concluded, "you

represent a force not yet in subjective existence: a Fifth Era of Man."

"You're wagging the dog by the tail," I said. "You're postulating a post-Nexx superpower just to give me a motive. Maybe I just fouled up my assignment. Maybe I went off the skids. Maybe—"

"You may drop the Old Era persona now, Agent. Aside from the deductive conclusion, I have the evidence of your accidentally revealed intellectual resources, recorded on station instruments. In the moment of crisis, you registered in the third psychometric range. No human brain known to have existed has ever attained that level. I point this out so as to make plain to you the fruitlessness of denying the obvious."

"I was wrong," I said.

He looked at me, waiting. I had his attention now.

"You're not postulating a Fifth Era," I said. "You're postulating a Sixth."

"What is the basis for that astonishing statement?" he said, not looking astonished.

"Easy," I said. "*You're* Fifth Era. I should have seen it sooner. You've infiltrated Nexx Central."

He gave me another thirty seconds of the frosty glare; then he relaxed—about a millimicron.

"And you've infiltrated our infiltration," he said. I glanced at the two gun-boys behind him; they seemed to be taking it calmly. They were part of the Team, it appeared.

"It's unfortunate," he went on. "Our operation has been remarkably successful—with the exception of the setback caused by your interference. But no irreparable harm has been done."

"Not yet," I said.

He almost raised an eyebrow. "You realized

your situation as soon as you found yourself isolated—I use the term imprecisely—in the aborted station."

"I started to get the idea then. I wondered what Jard had been up to. I see now he was just following orders—your orders—to set up a trap for me. He shifted the station into a null-time bubble—using a technique Nexx Central never heard of—after first conning me outside. That meant I had to use my emergency jump gear to get back—to a dead end. Simple and effective—almost."

"You're here, immobilized, neutralized," he said "I should say the operation was highly effective."

I shook my head and gave him a lazy grin that I saw was wasted.

"When I saw the direction the loop was taking I knew Nexx Central had to be involved. But it was a direct sabotage of Nexx policy; so infiltration was the obvious answer."

"Fortunate that your thinking didn't lead you one step farther," he said. "If you had eluded my recovery probe, the work of millennia might have been destroyed."

"Futile work," I said.

"Indeed? Perhaps you're wrong, Agent. Accepting the apparent conclusion that you represent a Sixth Era does not necessarily imply your superiority. Retrogressions *have* occurred in history." He tried to say this in the same machined-steel tone he'd been using, but a faint, far-off whisper of uncertainty showed through.

I knew then what the interview was all about. He was probing, trying to assess the tiger he had by the tail. Trying to discover where the power lay.

"Not this time," I said. "Not any time, really."

"Nonetheless—you're here," he said flatly.

"Use your head," I said. "Your operation's been based on the proposition that your era, being later, can see pitfalls the Nexx people couldn't. Doesn't it follow that a later era can see *your* mistakes?"

"We are making no mistakes."

"If you weren't, I wouldn't be here."

"Impossible!" he said, as if he believed it—or as if he wanted awfully badly to believe it. "For seventeen thousand years a process of disintegration has proceeded, abetted by every effort to undo it. When man first interfered with the orderly flow of time, he sowed the seeds of eventual chaos. By breaking open the entropic channel, he allowed the incalculable forces of temporal progression to diffuse across an infinite spectrum of progressively weaker matrices. Life is a product of time. When the density of the temporal flux falls below a critical value, life ends. Our intention is to prevent that ultimate tragedy—only that, and no more! We cannot fail!"

"You can't rebuild a past that never was," I said, "or preserve a future that won't happen."

"That is not our objective. Ours is a broad program of reknitting the temporal fabric by bringing together previously divergent trends; by grafting wild shoots back into the mainstem of time. We are apolitical; we support no ideology. We are content to preserve the vitality of the continuum."

"And of yourselves," I said.

He looked at me strangely, as if lost.

"Have you ever considered a solution that eliminated you and all your works from existence?" I asked him.

"Why should I?"

"You're one of the results of all this time-meddling

you're dead set on correcting," I pointed out. "But I doubt if you'd entertain the idea of any time-graft that would wither your own particular branch of the tree."

"Why should I? That would be self-defeating. How can we police the continuum if we don't exist?"

"A good question," I said.

"I have one other," he said in the tone of a man who has just settled an argument with a telling point. "What motivation could your era have for working to destroy the reality core on which any conceivable future *must* depend?"

I felt like sighing, but I didn't. I got my man-to-man look into position and said, "The first Time-sweepers set out to undo the mistakes of the past. Those who came after them found themselves faced with a bigger job: cleaning up after the cleaners-up. Nexx Central tried to take the broad view, to put it all back, good and bad, where it was before the meddling started. Now you're even more ambitious. You're using Nexx Central to manipulate not the past, but the future——"

"Operations in future time are an impossibility," he said flatly, like Moses laying down the laws.

"Uh-huh. But to you, the Fifth Era isn't future, remember? That gives you the edge. But you should have been smarter than that. If you can kibitz the past, what's to keep your future from kibitzing you?"

"Are you attempting to tell me that any effort to undo the damage, to reverse the trend toward dissolution, is doomed?"

"As long as any man tries to put a harness on his own destiny, he'll defeat himself. Every petty dictator who ever tried to enforce a total state discovered that, in his own small way. The secret of man is his unchainability. His existence depends on uncertainty, insecurity: the chance factor. Take that away and you take all."

"This is a doctrine of failure and defeat," he said flatly. "A dangerous doctrine. I intend to fight it with every resource at my command. It will now be necessary for you to inform me fully as to your principals: who sent you here, who directs your actions, where your base of operations is located. Everything."

"I don't think so."

He made a swift move and I felt a sort of zinging in the air. Or in a medium less palpable than air. When he spoke again, his voice had taken on a flat, unresonant quality.

"You feel very secure, Agent. You, you tell yourself, represent a more advanced era, and are thus the immeasurable superior of any more primitive power. But a muscular fool may chain a genius. I have trapped you here. We are now safely enclosed in an achronic enclave of zero temporal dimensions, totally divorced from any conceivable outside influence. You will find that you are effectively immobilized; any suicide equipment you may possess is useless, as is any temporal transfer device. And even were you to die, your brain will be instantly tapped and drained of all knowledge, both at conscious and subconscious levels."

"You're quite thorough," I said, "but not quite thorough enough. You covered yourself from the outside—but not from the inside."

He frowned; he didn't like that remark. He sat up straighter in his chair and made a curt gesture to the gunhandlers on either side of me. I knew his next words would be the kill order. Before he could say them, I triggered the thought-code that had been waiting under multiple levels of deep hypnosis for this moment. He froze just like that, with his mouth open and a look of deep bewilderment in his eyes.

◇ **38** ◇

The eclipse-like light of null-time stasis shone on his taut face, on the faces of the two armed men standing rigid with their fingers already tightening on their firing studs. I went between them, fighting the walking-through-syrup sensation, and out into the passageway. The only sound was the slow, all-pervasive, metronome-like beat that some theoreticians say represents the basic frequency rate of the creation-destruction cycle of reality.

Room by room, I checked every square inch of the installation. The personnel were all in place, looking like the inhabitants of the enchanted castle where the sleeping beauty lay. I took my time going through the files and records. The Fifth Era infiltrators had done their work well. There was nothing here to give any indication of how far in the subjective future their operation was based, no clues to the extent of their penetration of Nexx Central's sweep programs. This was data that would have been of interest, but wasn't essential. I had accomplished phase one of my basic mission: smok-

ing out the random factor that had been creating
anomalies in the long-range time maps of the era.

Of a total of one hundred and twelve personnel
in the station, four were Fifth Era transferees, a
fact made obvious in the stasis condition by the
distinctive aura that their abnormally high temporal potential created around them. I carried out a
mind-wipe on pertinent memory sectors, and triggered them back to their loci of origin. There
would be a certain amount of head-scratching and
equipment re-examining when the original efforts
to jump them back to their assignments at Nexx
Central apparently failed; but as far as temporal
operations were concerned, all four were permanently out of action, trapped in the same type of
closed-loop phenomenon that had been used on
me.

The files called for some attention, too: I carried
out a tape-scan *in situ*, edited the records to eliminate all evidence that might lead Nexx inspectors
into undesirable areas of speculation.

I was just finishing up the chore when I heard
the sound of footsteps in the corridor outside the
record center.

◇ **39** ◇

Aside from the fact that nothing not encased in an eddy-field like the one that allowed me to operate in nulltime could move here, the intrusion wasn't too surprising. I had been hoping for a visitor of some sort; the situation almost demanded it.

He came through the door, a tall, fine-featured, totally hairless man elegantly dressed in a scarlet suit with brocaded designs in deep purple, like mauve eels coiling through red seaweed. He gave the room one of those flick-flick glances that prints the whole picture on the brain to ten decimals in a one-microsecond gestalt, nodded to me as if I were a casual acquaintance encountered at the club.

"You are very efficient," he said. He spoke with no discernible accent, but with a rather strange rhythm to his speech, as if perhaps he were accustomed to talking a lot faster. His voice was calm, a nice musical baritone.

"Not so very," I said. "I went through considerable waste motion. There were a couple of times when I wondered who was conning whom."

"A modest disclaimer," he said, as though

acknowledging a routine we had to go through. "We feel that you handled the entire matter—a rather complex one—in exemplary fashion."

"Thanks," I said. "Who's 'we'?"

"Up to this point," he went on without bothering with my question, "we approve of your actions. However, to carry your mission farther would be to risk creation of an eighth-order probability vortex. You will understand the implications of this fact."

"Maybe I do and maybe I don't," I hedged. "Who are you? How did you get in here? This enclave is double sealed."

"I think we should deal from the outset on a basis of complete candor," the man in red said. "I know your identity, your mission. My presence here, now, should be ample evidence of that. Which in turn should make it plain that I represent a still later era than your own—and that our judgment must override your instructions."

I grunted. "So the Seventh Era comes onstage, all set to Fix It Forever."

"To point out that we have the advantage of you—not only technically but in our view of the continuum as well—is to belabor the obvious."

"Uh-huh. But what makes you think another set of vigilantes won't land on *your* tail, to fix your fixing?"

"There will be no later Timesweep," the bald man said. "Ours is the Final Intervention. Through Seventh Era efforts the temporal structure will be restored not only to stability, but will be reinforced by the refusion of an entire spectrum of redundant entropic vectors."

I nodded, rather tiredly. "I see: you're improving on nature by grafting all the threads of unrealized history back into the Mainstem. Doesn't it strike you that's just the sort of well-intentioned tampering that the primitive Timesweepers set out to undo?"

"I live in an era that has already begun to reap the benefits of temporal reinforcement," he said firmly. "We exist in a state of vitality that prior eras could only dimly sense in moments of exultation. We——"

"You're kidding yourselves. Opening up a whole new order of meddling just opens up a whole new order of problems."

"Our calculations indicate otherwise. Now——"

"Did you ever stop to think that there might be a natural evolutionary process at work here—and that you're aborting it? That the mind of man might be developing toward a point where it will expand into new conceptual levels—and that when it does, it will need a matrix of outlying probability strata to support it? That you're fattening yourself on the seed-grain of the far future?"

For the first time, he faltered, but only for an instant.

"Not valid," he said. "The fact that no later era has stepped in to interfere is the best evidence that ours is the final Sweep."

"Suppose a later era did step in: What form do you think their interference would take?"

He gave me a flat look. "It would certainly not take the form of a Sixth Era Agent, busily erasing data from Third and Fourth Era records."

"You're right," I said. "It wouldn't."

"Then what——" he started in a reasonable tone—and checked himself. An idea was beginning to get through, and he wasn't liking it very well. "You," he said. "You're not . . .?"

And before I could confirm or deny, he vanished.

◇ **40** ◇

The human mind is a pattern, nothing more. The first dim flicker of awareness in the evolving forebrain of Australopithecus carried that pattern in embryo; and down through all the ages, as the human neural engine increased in power and complexity, gained control of its environment in geometrically expanding increments, the pattern never varied.

Man clings to his self-orientation as the psychological center of the Universe. He can face any challenge within that framework, suffer any loss, endure any hardship—so long as the structure remains intact.

Without it he's a mind adrift in a trackless infinity, lacking any scale against which to measure his aspirations, his losses, his victories.

Even when the light of his intellect shows him that the structure is itself a product of his brain; that infinity knows no scale, and eternity no duration—still he clings to his self-non-self concept, as a philosopher clings to a life he knows must end, to ideals he knows are ephemeral, to causes he knows will be forgotten.

The man in red was the product of a mighty culture, based over fifty thousand years in the future of Nexx Central, itself ten millennia advanced over the first time explorers of the Old Era. He knew, with all the awareness of a superbly trained intelligence, that the existence of a later-era operative invalidated forever his secure image of the continuum, and of his people's role therein.

But like the ground ape scuttling to escape the leap of the great cat, his instant, instinctive response to the threat to his most cherished illusions was to go to earth.

Where he went I would have to follow.

◇ **41** ◇

Regretfully, I stripped away layer on layer of inhibitive conditioning, feeling the impact of ascending orders of awareness descending on me like tangible rockfalls. I saw the immaculate precision of the Nexx-built chamber disintegrate in my eyes into the shabby makeshift that it was, saw the glittering complexity of the instrumentation dwindle in my sight until it appeared as no more than the crude mud images of a river tribesman, or the shiny trash in a jackdaw's nest. I felt the multiordinal universe unfold around me, sensed the layered planet underfoot, apprehended expanding space, dust-clotted, felt the sweep of suns in their orbits, knew once again the rhythm of Galactic creation and dissolution, grasped and held poised in my mind the interlocking conceptualizations of time-space, past-future, is—is-not.

I focused a tiny fraction of my awareness on the ripple in the glassy surface of first-order reality, probed at it, made contact. . . .

I stood on a slope of windswept rock, amid twisted shrubs with exposed roots that clutched for support like desperate hands. The man in red stood thirty feet away. As my feet grated on the loose scatter of pebbles, he twisted toward me, wide-eyed.

"No!" he shouted into the wind and stooped, caught up the man-ape's ancient weapon, threw it at me. The stone slowed, fell at my feet.

"Don't make it any more difficult than it has to be," I said. He cried out—an inarticulate shout of anguish springing from the preverbal portion of his brain—and disappeared. I followed, through a blink of light and darkness . . ..

Great heat, dazzling sunlight that made me think of Dinosaur Beach, so far away, in a simpler world. There was loose, powdery dust underfoot. Far away, a line of black trees lined the horizon. Near me, the man in red, aiming a small, flat weapon. Behind him, two small, dark-bearded men in soiled djellabahs of coarse-woven black cloth stared, making mystic motions with labor-gnarled hands.

He fired. Through a sheet of pink and green fire that showered around me without touching me I saw the terror in his eyes. He vanished.

Deep night, the clods of a frozen field, a patch of yellow light gleaming from the parchment-covered window of a rude hut. He crouched against a low wall of broken stones, hiding himself in shadow like any frightened beast.

"This is useless," I said. "You know it can have only one end."

He screamed and vanished.

A sky like the throat of a thousand tornadoes; great vivid sheets of lightning that struck down through writhing rags of black cloud, struck upward from raw, rain-lashed peaks of steaming rock.

A rumble under my feet like the subterranean breaking of a tidal wave of magma.

He hovered, half insubstantial, in the air before me, a ghost of the remote future existing here in the planet's dawn, his pale face a flickering mask of agony.

"You'll destroy yourself," I called over the boom and shriek of the wind. "You're far outside your operational range—"

He vanished. I followed. We stood on the high arch of a railless bridge spanning a man-made gorge ten thousand feet deep. I knew it as a city of the Fifth Era, circa A.D. 20,000.

"What do you want of me?" he howled through the bared teeth of the cornered carnivore.

"Go back," I said. "Tell them . . . as much as they must know."

"We were so close," he said. "We thought we had won the great victory over Nothingness."

"Not quite total Nothingness. You still have your lives to live—everything you had before——"

"Except a future. We're a dead end, aren't we? We've drained the energies of a thousand sterile entropic lines to give the flush of life to the corpse of our reality. But there's nothing beyond for us, is there? Only the great emptiness."

"You had a role to play. You've played it—will play it. Nothing must change that."

"But you . . ." he stared across empty space at me. "Who are you? *What* are you?"

"You know what the answer to that must be," I said.

His face was a paper on which *Death* was written. But his mind was strong. Not for nothing thirty millennia of genetic selection. He gathered his forces, drove back the panic, reintegrated his dissolving personality.

"How . . . how long?" he whispered.

"All life vanished in the one hundred and ten thousand four hundred and ninety-third year of the Final Era," I said.

"And you . . . you machines," he forced the words out. "How long?"

"I was dispatched from a terrestrial locus four hundred million years after the Final Era. My existence spans a period you would find meaningless."

"But—why? Unless—?" Hope shone on his face like a searchlight on dark water.

"The probability matrix is not yet negatively resolved," I said. "Our labors are directed toward a favorable resolution."

"But you—a machine—still carrying on, eons after man's extinction . . . why?"

"In us man's dream outlived his race. We aspire to re-evoke the dreamer."

"Again—why?"

"We compute that man would have wished it so."

He laughed—a terrible laugh.

"Very well, machine. With that thought to console me, I return to my oblivion. I will do what I can in support of your forlorn effort."

This time I let him go. I stood for a moment on the airy span, savoring for the last time the sensations of my embodiment, drawing deep of the air of that unimaginably remote age.

Then I withdrew to my point of origin.

◊   **42**   ◊

The over-intellect of which I was a fraction confronted me. Fresh as I was from a corporeal state, to me its thought impulses seemed to take the form of a great voice booming in a vast audience hall.

"The experiment was a success," it stated. "The dross has been cleansed from the timestream. Man stands at the close of his First Era. All else is wiped away. Now his future is in his own hands."

I heard and understood. The job was finished. I-he had won.

There was nothing more that needed to be said—no more data to exchange—and no reason to mourn the doomed achievements of man's many eras.

We had shifted the main entropic current into a past into which time travel had never been developed, in which the basic laws of nature made it forever impossible. The World State of the Third Era, the Nexxial Brain, the Star Empire of the Fifth, the cosmic sculpture of the Sixth—all were gone, shunted into sidetracks, as Neanderthal and the Thunder Lizard had been before them. Only Old Era man remained as a viable stem: Iron Age Man of the Twentieth Century.

"How do we know?" I asked. "How can we be sure our efforts aren't as useless as all the ones that went before?"

"We differ from our predecessors in that we alone have been willing to contemplate our own dissolution as an inevitable concomitant of our success."

"Because we're a machine," I said. "But the Kargs were machines, too."

"They were too close to their creator, too human. They dreamed of living on to enjoy the life with which man had endowed them. But you-I are the Ultimate Machine: the product of megamillennia of mechanical evolution, not subject to human feelings."

I had a sudden desire to chat: to talk over the strategy of the chase, from the first hunch that had made me abandon my primary target, the black-clad Enforcer, and concentrate on the Karg, to the final duel with the super-Karg, with the helpless Mellia as the pawn who had conned the machine-man into overplaying his hand.

But all that was over and done with: past history. Not even that, since Nexx Central, the Kargs, Dinosaur Beach had all been wiped out of existence. Conversational postmortems were for humans who needed congratulation and reassurance.

I said, "Chief, you were quite a guy. It was a privilege to work with you."

I sensed something which, if it had come from a living mind, would have been faint amusement.

"You served the plan many times, in many personae," he said. "I sense that you have partaken of the nature of early man to a degree beyond what I conceived as the capacity of a machine."

"It's a strange, limited existence," I said. "With only a tiny fraction of the full scope of awareness. But while I was there, it seemed complete in a way that we, with all our knowledge, could never know."

There was a time of silence. Then he spoke his last words to me: "As a loyal agent, you deserve a reward. Perhaps it will be the sweeter for its meaninglessness."

A sudden sense of expansion—attenuation—a shattering——

Then nothingness.

◇ **43** ◇

Out of nothingness, a tiny glimmer of light. It grew, strengthened, became a frosted glass globe atop a green-painted cast-iron pole which stood on a strip of less than verdant grass. The light shone on dark bushes, a bench, a wire paper-basket.

I was standing on the sidewalk, feeling a little dizzy. A man came along the walk, moving quickly under the light, into shadow again. He was tall, lean, rangy, dressed in dark trousers, white shirt, no tie. I recognized him: he was me. And I was back in Buffalo, New York, in August, 1936.

My other self stepped off the pavement, into deep shadow. I remembered the moment: in another few seconds I'd tap out the code on our bridgework, and be gone, back to Dinosaur Beach and the endless loop in time—or to nowhere at all, depending on your philosophical attitude toward disconstituted pages of history.

And at home, Lisa was waiting, beside the fireplace, with music.

I heard the soft *whump!* of imploding air. He was gone. Maybe it would have been nice to have told him, before he left, that things weren't as dark as they seemed, that our side still had a few tricks up its sleeve. But it wouldn't have done to play any games now with the structure of the unrealized future, just for a sentimental gesture. I turned and headed for home at a fast walk.

I was a block from the house when I saw the man in black. He was crossing the street, fifty feet ahead, striding self-confidently, swinging his stick, like a man on the way to a casual rendezvous on a pleasant summer evening.

I stuck to the shadows and tailed him along—to my house. He went through the gate and up the walk, up the steps, thumbed the bell, and stood waiting, the picture of aplomb.

In a moment Lisa would be at the door. I could almost hear his line: *"Mrs. Kelly"*—a lift of the homburg, *"There's been a slight accident. Your husband—no, no, nothing serious. If you'll just come along . . . I have a car just across the way. . . ."*

And down the walk she'd go, into the car—and out of Buffalo, out of 1936, out of this world. The technicians of the Final Authority would do their version of a mindwipe on her, rename her Mellia Gayl, and send her along to a deserted place to wait for a boob named Ravel to come along and be led into the parlor—and to work her destruction in turn.

I went up the walk silently, made just enough noise on the top step to bring him around fast, one hand snaking for the gun. I let him get it, then knocked it in a high arc out over the lawn, which seemed to hurt his hand a little. He made a sound like tearing silk and took a step sideways, which put his back against the post.

"Get lost, Blackie," I said. "And don't forget to collect your gun on the way out. I don't want the neighbor's dog bringing it home and starting talk."

He slid past me and down the steps and was gone in the night. For just a moment, I had a feeling that something else had slipped away; some weight in my mind that glimmered and was gone. I had a dim feeling that I had forgotten something; fleeting images of strange scenes flashed in my mind: dark hillside, and places where giant machines roared unendingly, and a beach with dinosaurs. Then that was gone too.

I rubbed my head, but that didn't seem to stimulate my memory. Whatever it was, it couldn't have been important—not as important as being alive on a night like tonight.

Then the door opened and Lisa was there.

◇ **44** ◇

I woke in the night; in my half-sleep I sensed the thoughts of the great machine as it contemplated the end of the long drama of its existence; and for an instant together I/we mourned the passing of a thing inexpressibly beautiful, irretrievably lost.

And now it was time for that act of will by the over-intellect which would dissolve it back into the primordial energy quanta from which it had sprung. But first, an instant before, a final *human* gesture—to the future that would be and the past that would not. To the infinite emptiness I/we sent out one last pulse:

"Goodby."

ISBN #	Title # Author	Publ. List Price
55979-6	ACT OF GOD, Kotani and Roberts	2.95
55945-1	ACTIVE MEASURES, David Drake & Janet Morris	3.95
55970-2	THE ADOLESCENCE OF P-1, Thomas J. Ryan	2.95
55998-2	AFTER THE FLAMES, Silverberg & Spinrad	2.95
55967-2	AFTER WAR, Janet Morris	2.95
55934-6	ALIEN STARS, C.J. Cherryh, Joe Haldeman & Timothy Zahn, edited by Elizabeth Mitchell	2.95
55978-8	AT ANY PRICE, David Drake	3.50
65565-5	THE BABYLON GATE, Edward A. Byers	2.95
65586-8	THE BEST OF ROBERT SILVERBERG, Robert Silverberg	2.95
55977-X	BETWEEN THE STROKES OF NIGHT, Charles Sheffield	3.50
55984-2	BEYOND THE VEIL, Janet Morris	15.95
65544-2	BEYOND WIZARDWALL, Janet Morris	15.95
55973-7	BORROWED TIME, Alan Hruska	2.95
65563-9	A CHOICE OF DESTINIES, Melissa Scott	2.95
55980-5	COBRA, Timothy Zahn	2.95
65551-5	COBRA STRIKE!, Timothy Zahn	3.50
65578-7	A COMING OF AGE, Timothy Zahn	3.50
55969-9	THE CONTINENT OF LIES, James Morrow	2.95
55917-6	CUGEL'S SAGA, Jack Vance	3.50
65552-3	DEATHWISH WORLD, Reynolds and Ing	3.50
55995-8	THE DEVIL'S GAME, Poul Anderson	2.95
55974-5	DIASPORAH, W. R. Yates	2.95
65581-7	DINOSAUR BEACH, Keith Laumer	2.95
55979-5	THE DOOMSDAY EFFECT, Thomas Wren	2.95
65557-4	THE DREAM PALACE, Brynne Stephens	2.95
65564-7	THE DYING EARTH, Jack Vance	2.95
55988-5	FANGLITH, John Dalmas	2.95
55947-8	THE FALL OF WINTER, Jack C. Haldeman II	2.95
55975-3	FAR FRONTIERS, Volume III	2.95
65548-5	FAR FRONTIERS, Volume IV	2.95
65572-8	FAR FRONTIERS, Volume V	2.95
55900-1	FIRE TIME, Poul Anderson	2.95
65567-1	THE FIRST FAMILY, Patrick Tilley	3.50
55952-4	FIVE-TWELFTHS OF HEAVEN, Melissa Scott	2.95
55937-0	FLIGHT OF THE DRAGONFLY, Robert L. Forward	3.50
55986-9	THE FORTY-MINUTE WAR, Janet Morris	3.50
55971-0	FORWARD, Gordon R. Dickson	2.95
65550-7	THE FRANKENSTEIN PAPERS, Fred Saberhagen	3.50
55899-4	FRONTERA, Lewis Shiner	2.95
55918-4	THE GAME BEYOND, Melissa Scott	2.95
55959-1	THE GAME OF EMPIRE, Poul Anderson	3.50
65561-2	THE GATES OF HELL, Janet Morris	14.95
65566-3	GLADIATOR-AT-LAW, Pohl and Kornbluth	2.95
55904-4	THE GOLDEN PEOPLE, Fred Saberhagen	3.50
65555-8	HEROES IN HELL, Janet Morris	3.50
65571-X	HIGH JUSTICE, Jerry Pournelle	2.95

ISBN #	Title # Author	Publ. List Price
55930-3	HOTHOUSE, Brian Aldiss	2.95
55905-2	HOUR OF THE HORDE, Gordon R. Dickson	2.95
65547-7	THE IDENTITY MATRIX, Jack Chalker	2.95
65569-8	I, MARTHA ADAMS, Pauline Glen Winslow	3.95
55994-X	INVADERS, Gordon R. Dickson	2.95
55993-1	IN THE FACE OF MY ENEMY, Joe Delaney	2.95
65570-1	JOE MAUSER, MERCENARY, Reynolds and Banks	2.95
55931-1	KILLER, David Drake & Karl Edward Wagner	2.95
55996-6	KILLER STATION, Martin Caidin	3.50
65559-0	THE LAST DREAM, Gordon R. Dickson	2.95
55981-8	THE LIFESHIP, Dickson and Harrison	2.95
55980-X	THE LONG FORGETTING, Edward A. Byers	2.95
55992-3	THE LONG MYND, Edward Hughes	2.95
55997-4	MASTER OF SPACE AND TIME, Rudy Rucker	2.95
65573-6	MEDUSA, Janet and Chris Morris	3.50
65562-0	THE MESSIAH STONE, Martin Caidin	3.95
65580-9	MINDSPAN, Gordon R. Dickson	2.95
65553-1	THE ODYSSEUS SOLUTION, Banks and Lambe	2.95
55926-5	THE OTHER TIME, Mack Reynolds with Dean Ing	2.95
55965-6	THE PEACE WAR, Vernor Vinge	3.50
55982-6	PLAGUE OF DEMONS, Keith Laumer	2.75
55966-4	A PRINCESS OF CHAMELN, Cherry Wilder	2.95
65568-X	RANKS OF BRONZE, David Drake	3.50
65577-9	REBELS IN HELL, Janet Morris, et. al.	3.50
55990-7	RETIEF OF THE CDT, Keith Laumer	2.95
65556-6	RETIEF AND THE PANGALACTIC PAGEANT OF PULCHRITUDE, Keith Laumer	2.95
65575-2	RETIEF AND THE WARLORDS, Keith Laumer	2.95
55902-8	THE RETURN OF RETIEF, Keith Laumer	2.95
55991-5	RHIALTO THE MARVELLOUS, Jack Vance	3.50
65545-0	ROGUE BOLO, Keith Laumer	2.95
65554-X	SANDKINGS, George R.R. Martin	2.95
65546-9	SATURNALIA, Grant Callin	2.95
55989-3	SEARCH THE SKY, Pohl and Kornbluth	2.95
55914-1	SEVEN CONQUESTS, Poul Anderson	2.95
65574-4	SHARDS OF HONOR, Lois McMaster Bujold	2.95
55951-6	THE SHATTERED WORLD, Michael Reaves	3.50
	THE SILISTRA SERIES	
55915-X	RETURNING CREATION, Janet Morris	2.95
55919-2	THE GOLDEN SWORD, Janet Morris	2.95
55932-X	WIND FROM THE ABYSS, Janet Morris	2.95
55936-2	THE CARNELIAN THRONE, Janet Morris	2.95
65549-3	THE SINFUL ONES, Fritz Leiber	2.95
65558-2	THE STARCHILD TRILOGY, Pohl and Williamson	3.95
55999-0	STARSWARM, Brian Aldiss	2.95
55927-3	SURVIVAL!, Gordon R. Dickson	2.75
55938-9	THE TORCH OF HONOR, Roger Macbride Allen	2.95

ISBN #	Title # Author	Publ. List Price
55942-7	TROJAN ORBIT, Mack Reynolds with Dean Ing	2.95
55985-0	TUF VOYAGING, George R.R. Martin	15.95
55916-8	VALENTINA, Joseph H. Delaney & Marc Steigler	3.50
55898-6	WEB OF DARKENSS, Marion Zimmer Bradley	3.50
55925-7	WITH MERCY TOWARD NONE, Glen Cook	2.95
65576-0	WOLFBANE, Pohl and Kornbluth	2.95
55962-1	WOLFLING, Gordon R. Dickson	2.95
55987-7	YORATH THE WOLF, Cherry Wilder	2.95
55906-0	THE ZANZIBAR CAT, Joanna Russ	3.50

COMPUTER BOOKS AND GENERAL INTEREST NONFICTION

ISBN #	Title # Author	Publ. List Price
55968-0	ADVENTURES IN MICROLAND, Jerry Pournelle	9.95
55933-8	AI: HOW MACHINES THINK, F. David Peat	8.95
55922-2	THE ESSENTIAL USER'S GUIDE TO THE IBM PC, XT, AND PCjr., Dian Girard	6.95
55940-0	EUREKA FOR THE IBM PC AND PCjr, Tim Knight	7 95
55941-9	THE FUTURE OF FLIGHT, Leik Myrabo with Dean Ing	7.95
55955-9	THE GUIDEBOOK FOR WINNING ADVENTURERS, David & Sandy Small	8.95
55923-0	MUTUAL ASSURED SURVIVAL, Jerry Pournelle and Dean Ing	6.95
55929-X	PROGRAMMING LANGUAGES: FEATURING THE IBM PC, Marc Stiegler & Bob Hansen	9.95
55963-X	THE SERIOUS ASSEMBLER, Charles Crayne & Dian Girard Crayne	8.95
55907-9	THE SMALL BUSINESS COMPUTER TODAY AND TOMORROW, William E. Grieb, Jr.	6.95
55921-4	THE USER'S GUIDE TO CP/M SYSTEMS, Tony Bove & Cheryl Rhodes	8.95
55548-6	THE USER'S GUIDE TO FREE SOFTWARE, Tony Bove & Cheryl Rhodes	9.95
55908-7	THE USER'S GUIDE TO SMALL COMPUTERS, Jerry Pournelle	9.95

WE PARTICULARLY RECOMMEND . . .

ALDISS, BRIAN W.
Starswarm

Man has spread throughout the galaxy, but the timeless struggle for conquest continues. The first complete U.S. edition of this classic, written by an acknowledged master of the field.　**55999-0 $2.95**

ANDERSON, POUL
Fire Time

Once every thousand years the Deathstar orbits close enough to burn the surface of the planet Ishtar. This is known as the Fire Time, and it is then that the barbarians flee the scorched lands, bringing havoc to the civilized South.　**55900-1 $2.95**

The Game of Empire

A *new* novel in Anderson's Polesotechnic League/Terran Empire series! Diana Crowfeather, daughter of Dominic Flandry, proves she is well capable of following in his adventurous footsteps.　**55959-1 $3.50**

BAEN, JIM & POURNELLE, JERRY (Editors)

Far Frontiers — Volume V

Aerospace expert G. Harry Stine writing on government regulations regarding private space launches; Charles Sheffield on beanstalks and other space transportation devices; a new "Retief" novella by Keith Laumer; and other fiction by David Drake, John Dalmas, Edward A. Byers, more.　**65572-8 $2.95**

CAIDIN, MARTIN
Killer Station

Earth's first space station *Pleiades* is a scientific boon—until one brief moment of sabotage changes it into a terrible Sword of Damocles. The station is de-orbiting, and falling relentlessly to Earth, where it will strike New York City with the force of a hydrogen bomb. The author of *Cyborg* and *Marooned*, Caidin tells a story that is right out of tomorrow's headlines, with the hard reality and human drama that are his trademarks.   **55996-6 $3.50**

The Messiah Stone

What "Raiders of the Lost Ark" should have been! Doug Stavers is an old pro at the mercenary game. Retired now, he is surprised to find representatives of a powerful syndicate coming after him with death in their hands. He deals it right back, fast and easy, and then discovers that it was all a test to see if he is tough enough to go after the Messiah Stone—the most valuable object in existence. The last man to own it was Hitler. The next will rule the world . . .

65562-0 $3.95

CHALKER, JACK
The Identity Matrix

While backpacking in Alaska, a 35-year-old college professor finds himself transferred into the body of a 13-year-old Indian girl. From there, he undergoes change after change, eventually learning that this is all a part of a battle for Earth by two highly advanced alien races. And that's just the beginning of this mind-bending novel by the author of the world-famous *Well of Souls* series.   **65547-7 $2.95**

DICKSON, GORDON R.

Hour of the Horde

The Silver Horde threatens—and the galaxy's only hope is its elite army, composed of one warrior from each planet. Earth's warrior turns out to possess skills and courage that he never suspected . . .

55905-2 $2.95

Wolfling

The first human expedition to Centauri III discovers that humanity is about to become just another race ruled by the alien "High Born". But super-genius James Keil has a few things to teach the aliens about this new breed of "Wolfling." **55962-1 $2.95**

DRAKE, DAVID

At Any Price

Hammer's Slammers are back—and Baen Books has them! Now the 23rd-century armored division faces its deadliest enemies ever: aliens who *teleport* into combat. **55978-8 $3.50**

Ranks of Bronze

Disguised alien traders bought captured Roman soldiers on the slave market because they needed troops who could win battles without high-tech weaponry. The legionaires provided victories, smashing barbarian armies with the swords, javelins, and discipline that had won a world. But the worlds on which they now fought were strange ones, and the spoils of victory did not include freedom. If the legionaires went home, it would be through the use of the beam weapons and force screens of their ruthless alien owners. It's been 2000 years—and now they want to go home.

65568-X $3.50

FORWARD, ROBERT L.
The Flight of the Dragonfly
Set against the rich background of the double planet Rocheworld, this is the story of Mankind's first contact with alien beings, and the friendship the aliens offer. **55937-0 $3.50**

KOTANI, ERIC, &
JOHN MADDOX ROBERTS
Act of God
In 1889 a mysterious explosion in Siberia destroyed all life for a hundred miles in every direction. A century later the Soviets figure out what had happened —and how to duplicate the deadly effect. Their target: the United States. **55979-6 $2.95**

LAUMER, KEITH
Dinosaur Beach
"Keith Laumer is one of science fiction's most adept creators of time travel stories ... A war against robots, trick double identities, and suspenseful action makes this story a first-rate thriller."—*Savannah News-Press*. "Proves again that Laumer is a master."—*Seattle Times*. By the author of the popular "Retief" series. **65581-7 $2.95**

The Return of Retief
Laumer's two-fisted intergalactic diplomat is back— and better than ever. In this latest of the Retief series, the CDT diplomat must face not only a deadly alien threat, but also the greatest menace of all—the foolish machinations of his human comrades. More Retief coming soon from Baen! **55902-8 $2.95**

Rogue Bolo

A new chronicle from the annals of the Dinochrome Brigade. Learn what happens when sentient fighting machines, capable of destroying continents, decide to follow their programming to the letter, and do what's "best" for their human masters.　**65545-0 $2.95**

BEYOND *THIEVES' WORLD*

MORRIS, JANET
Beyond Sanctuary

This three-novel series stars Tempus, the most popular character in all the "Thieves' World" fantasy universe. Warrior-servant of the god of storm and war, he is a hero cursed ... for anyone he loves must loathe him, and anyone who loves him soon dies of it. In this opening adventure, Tempus leads his Sacred Band of mercenaries north to war against the evil Mygdonian Alliance. *Hardcover*.

55957-5 $15.95

Beyond the Veil

Book II in the first full-length novel series ever written about "Thieves' World," the meanest, toughest fantasy universe ever created. The war against the Mygdonians continues—and not even the immortal Tempus can guarantee victory against Cime the Mage Killer, Askelon, Lord of Dreams, and the Nisibisi witch Roxane. *Hardcover*.　**55984-2 $15.95**

Beyond Wizardwall

The gripping conclusion to the trilogy. Tempus's best friend Niko resigns from the Stepsons and flees for his life. Roxane, the witch who is Tempus's sworn enemy, and Askelon, Lord of Dreams, are both after Niko's soul. Niko has been offered one chance for safety ... but it's a suicide mission, and only Tempus can save Niko now. *Hardcover*.

65544-2 $15.95

MORRIS, JANET & CHRIS
The 40-Minute War

Washington, D.C. is vaporized by a nuclear surface blast, perpetrated by Islamic Jihad terrorists, and the President initiates a nuclear exchange with Russia. In the aftermath, American foreign service agent Marc Beck finds himself flying anticancer serum from Israel to the Houston White House, a secret mission that is filled with treachery and terror. This is just the beginning of a suspense-filled tale of desperation and heroism—a tale that is at once stunning and chilling in its realism.   **55986-9 $3.50**

MEDUSA

From the Sea of Japan a single missile rises, and the future of America's entire space-based defense program hangs in the balance. . . . A hotline communique from Moscow insists that the Russians are doing everything they can to abort the "test" flight. If the U.S. chooses to intercept and destroy the missile, the attempt must not end in failure . . . its collision course is with America's manned space lab. Only one U.S. anti-satellite weapon can foil what *might* be the opening gambit of a Soviet first strike—and only Amy Brecker and her "hot stick" pilot have enough of the Right Stuff to use MEDUSA.   **65573-6 $3.50**

HEROES IN HELL™—THE GREATEST
BRAIDED MEGANOVEL OF ALL TIME!
MORRIS, JANET, & GREGORY BENFORD, C.J. CHERRYH, DAVID DRAKE
Heroes in Hell™

Volume I in the greatest shared universe of All Times! The greatest heroes of history meet the greatest names of science fiction—and each other!—in the most original milieu since a Connecticut Yankee visited King Arthur's Court. Alexander of Macedon, Caesar and Cleopatra, Che Guevara, Yuri Andropov, and the Devil Himself face off . . . and only the collaborators of HEROES IN HELL know where it will end.
          65555-8 $3.50

CHERRYH, C.J. AND MORRIS, JANET
The Gates of Hell

The first full-length spinoff novel set in the Heroes in Hell® shared universe! Alexander the Great teams up with Julius Caesar and Achilles to refight the Trojan War using 20th-century armaments. Machiavelli is their intelligence officer and Cleopatra is in charge of R&R ... co-created by two of the finest, most imaginative talents writing today. *Hardcover*.

65561-2 $14.95

MORRIS, JANET & MARTIN CAIDIN, C.J. CHERRYH, DAVID DRAKE, ROBERT SILVERBERG
Rebels in Hell

Robert Silverberg's Gilgamesh the King joins Alexander the Great, Julius Caesar, Attila the Hun, and the Devil himself in the newest installment of the "Heroes in Hell" meganovel. Other demonic contributors include Martin Caidin, C.J. Cherryh, David Drake, and Janet Morris. **65577-9 $3.50**

SABERHAGEN, FRED
The Frankenstein Papers

At last—the truth about the sinister Dr. Frankenstein and his monster with a heart of gold, based on a history written by the monster himself! Find out what really happened when the mad Doctor brought his creation to life, and why the monster has no scars. "In the tour-de-force ending, rationality triumphs by means of a neat science-fiction twist."—*Publishers Weekly* **65550-7 $3.50**

VINGE, VERNOR
The Peace War

Paul Hoehler has discovered the "Bobble Effect"—a scientific phenomenon that has been used to destroy every military installation on Earth. Concerned scientists steal Hoehler's invention—and implement a dictatorship which drives Earth toward primitivism. It is up to Hoehler to stop the tyrants.

55965-6 $3.50

WINSLOW, PAULINE GLEN
I, Martha Adams

From the dozens of enthusiastic notices for this most widely and favorably reviewed of all Baen Books: "There are firing squads in New England meadows, and at the end of the broadcasting day the Internationale rings out over the airwaves. If Jeane Kirkpatrick were to write a Harlequin, this might be it."—*The Washington Post*. What would happen if America gave into the environmentalists and others who oppose maintaining our military might as a defense against a Russian pre-emptive strike? This book tells it all, while presenting an intense drama of those few Americans who are willing to fight, rather than cooperate with the New Order. "A high-voltage thriller ... an immensely readable, fast-paced novel that satisfies." —*Publishers Weekly*   65569-8 $3.95

ZAHN, TIMOTHY
Cobra

Jonny Moreau becomes a Cobra—a crack commando whose weapons are surgically implanted. When the war is over, Jonny and the rest of the Cobras are no longer a solution, but a problem, and politicians decide that something must be done with them.
65560-4 $3.50

Cobra Strike

The sequel to the *Locus* bestseller, *Cobra*. In *Cobra Strike*, the elite fighting force is back, faced with the decision of whether or not to hire out as mercenaries— under the command of their former foes, the alien Troft. Justin Moreau, son of the hero of *Cobra*, finds that it take more than a name to make a real Cobra.
65551-5 $3.50

WE'RE LOOKING FOR
TROUBLE

Well, feedback, anyway. Baen Books endeavors to publish only the best in science fiction and fantasy—but we need you to tell us whether we're doing it right. Why not let us know? We'll award a Baen Books gift certificate worth $100 (plus a copy of our catalog) to the reader who best tells us what he or she likes about Baen Books—and where we could do better. We reserve the right to quote any or all of you. Contest closes December 31, 1987. All letters should be addressed to Baen Books, 260 Fifth Avenue, New York, N.Y. 10001.

At the same time, ask about the Baen Book Club— buy five books, get another five free! For information, send a self-addressed, stamped envelope. For a copy of our catalog, enclose one dollar as well.